Teetoncey
and
Ben O'Neal

Teetoncey and Ben O'Neal

Theodore Taylor

An Odyssey/Harcourt Young Classic

Harcourt, Inc.

Orlando   Austin   New York   San Diego   Toronto   London

www.HarcourtBooks.com

First Harcourt Young Classics edition 2004
First Odyssey Classics edition 2004
First published by Doubleday and Company, Inc. 1975
First paperback edition published by Avon Books 1976

Library of Congress Cataloging-in-Publication Data
Taylor, Theodore, 1921–
Teetoncey and Ben O'Neal/by Theodore Taylor.
p. cm.
"The Cape Hatteras Trilogy."
Sequel to: Teetoncey.
Summary: When the English girl Ben saved from a shipwreck
recovers her memory and speech and reveals to him that two
chests full of silver went down with the ship, Ben and his friends
try to recover them without arousing suspicions.
[1. Outer Banks, N.C.—Fiction.   2. Buried treasure—Fiction.]   I. Title.
PZ7.T2186Tf   2004
[Fic]—dc22   2003067700
ISBN 0-15-205296-8
ISBN 0-15-205297-6 pb

Text set in Dante
Designed by Lydia D'moch

Printed in the United States of America

A C E G H F D B
A C E G H F D B (pb)

To Pete Glazer
Good newspaperman, good teacher, good friend

Laguna Beach, California
June 1974

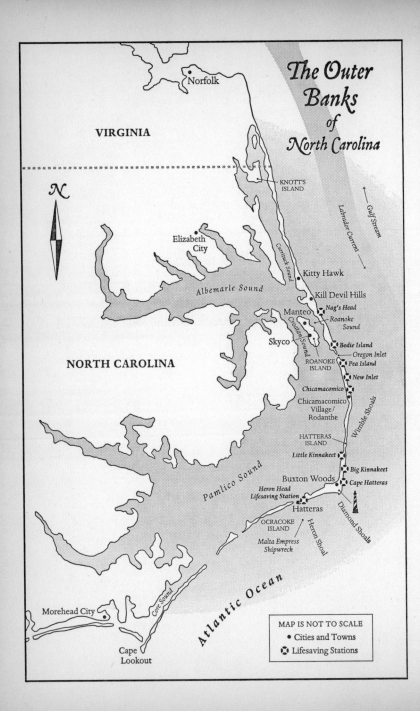

The Outer Banks of North Carolina

VIRGINIA

Norfolk

KNOTT'S ISLAND

Labrador Current

Gulf Stream

Elizabeth City

Kitty Hawk

Kill Devil Hills

Nag's Head

Manteo

Roanoke Sound

Skyco

Bodie Island

Oregon Inlet

ROANOKE ISLAND

Pea Island

NORTH CAROLINA

New Inlet

Chicamacomico

Chicamacomico Village / Rodanthe

Wimble Shoals

HATTERAS ISLAND

Little Kinnakeet

Big Kinnakeet

Buxton Woods

Cape Hatteras

Heron Head Lifesaving Station

Pamlico Sound

Hatteras

OCRACOKE ISLAND

Diamond Shoals

Heron Shoal

Malta Empress Shipwreck

Core Sound

Morehead City

Atlantic Ocean

Cape Lookout

MAP IS NOT TO SCALE
- Cities and Towns
- Lifesaving Stations

Albemarle Sound

Currituck Sound

Croatan Sound

Teetoncey
and
Ben O'Neal

I

ALTHOUGH THESE INCIDENTS happened long ago, I clearly remember feeling the fool, standing there with tears on my cheeks just because the British castaway had found her tongue instead of always staring at me as if I were a beach ghostie. In truth, *she* was the sand ghostie or had been.

This many years later, I still cannot say why I wept, which is not a manly thing to do, be you twelve or twenty-four. Perhaps it was because I had figured she was a hopeless orphan vegetable with addled brains and no tongue—then suddenly, she was cured; could think and speak.

Perhaps it was because I cared more about her than I ever allowed myself to admit. Whyever the reason, I felt the pure watery-eyed fool.

Just a few minutes later, about eight-thirty of that same stormy night, I also recollect that Mama rose from the girl's bedside and said to me, "Ben, you talk to the Mistress Appleton while I git a drop o' Purple."

She smiled down on the pale castaway. "That'll make you sleep like a warm stone." Then Mama padded off on her gray felt slippers, which she usually wore after sundown.

Something struck me. The *Mistress Appleton?* That sounded like we had somebody important in the house. Never before had I heard Mama call any ungrown female a "mistress." In fact, up to the previous hour, when I had forced the London girl to face the gale and roaring surf, we'd called her *Teetoncey* simply because we hadn't known her true name. The word means small of any amount on our Outer Banks of North Carolina.

It would take some proper attention, I recall thinking, to implant the new name of Wendy

Lynn Appleton in my mind. But that wasn't the problem at the moment. I didn't exactly know what to say to her.

Having wiped away those embarrassing tears, still thoroughly uncomfortable, I finally managed, rocking on my seaboots about six feet from her, "Gale'll be over soon."

The wind was already losing its high whine, shifting more to due east than north after its quick smite at our Cape Hatteras coast. Midnight would see it down to a sigh.

Nodding slightly, but now evidently disinterested in both the weather and me, the girl, her skin flour white from the evening's very unusual ordeal, eyes dull from shock, turned her daisy head toward the window though there wasn't much to see out there through the beading lances of water on the panes. The streaks glistened in the soft orange reflection of the table lamp.

Boo Dog, my gold hound, a Labrador by breed, rose up slowly from the oval rag rug, curved his back in luxury, and then moved to the other side of the bed and wisely put his head in a position to be stroked. The girl took a hand from beneath the crazy-patch comforter and began to rub his scalp, though she didn't seem to be aware she was doing it. She knew him better than she thought.

But it was quite obvious to me that she didn't want to talk to anyone at the moment and I could certainly understand why. Only survivor of the wrecked barkentine *Malta Empress*, she had been mauled by the sea, smacking her head on the bottom, blocking her mind for twenty-eight perplexing days. Yet now that she'd come out of her mental darkness and silence, I desperately wanted to hear all about that shipwreck. Perhaps on the morrow she'd say how it all happened. Her story would be of interest to everyone on the Carolina Banks since wrecks were our heritage.

Mama came back with a jelly glass, filled halfway with the milky-purple liquid. A single dollop of that sticky medicine, kept in a small vial in the kitchen, was enough for sweet dreams. It was another of my older brother Reuben's contributions from his various voyages, and was said to be opium and something else, up from a Chinese shopkeeper in Trinidad. It worked, as I could testify.

Mama sat down on the bed's edge as the girl turned her head from the window. Mama said, softly and cheerfully, "Now, take this in one long gulp an' the morrow'll be a brighter day."

The girl swallowed it and then dropped her head back to the pillow, closing her red-rimmed eyes, and returning her small hand under the comforter.

Face soft as lamb's belly, full of tenderness and concern, Mama said, "We'll jus' visit silent till you steal off."

Not a peep was made by the girl.

The ship's clock in the living room ticked on and the wind outside settled lower to a strum. There was no other sound in our cottage tucked back in a hammock not too far from Heron Head Shoal. Distantly, the surf crashed on the beach. I even muted my breath, watching the face with the pointed nose relax and sag into Purple peace.

Soon Mama nodded and we eased out of the pine-board room which had been my own for years; leaving the door open and the oil lamp aglow.

We lit another lamp and went into the kitchen. Mama rinsed the medicine glass in the wooden sink bucket and then sighed tiredly. December 5, 1898, was a wearing night. "Think I'll put some tea on, Ben," she said. The yaupon tea, made from holly, was her defense against harassment, natural and otherwise. Whiskey and wine never touched the lips of Rachel O'Neal. She was as good a Methodist woman as I have ever known.

I sat down at the table. "What'd she say about the wreck?"

"Not much."

"But, Mama, you were in there for almost an hour before you called me in."

"Ben, the child come out o' shock. She didn't know who she was; who we were. She hadn't remembered a thing till this night. I wasn't concerned about no shipwreck. I asked no questions."

"Well, she must have said something."

"I have an ideer she'll say it all later."

There had been very little schooling on the Banks when Mama was a girl, born 1848, and her grammar lacked. She said "git" and "ideer" and other things, but all the old people spoke much the same way. Mainlanders sometimes considered us ignorant and quaint, especially when some of us said "hoigh" for *high* and "toide" for *tide* and "oiland" for *island* and "loight" for *light,* but that's the way it was.

Jabez Tillett might say, for instance, "The toide is hoigh at Body Oiland." And that would be "foine" with everyone. Or Rasmus Gaskill, who liked his nip of Moyock corn likker, might say, "When oi git too toight, oi clim' up an' down the steps o' the loight three toimes an' oi'm sober."

Some of us talked that way but not all of us. Some said our dialect came from London cockneys, the lower classes; others said it was from Devon, also in England. It wasn't worth any argument.

Mama carried the kettle into the front room and put it on top of our heating stove, which was shaped like a fat iron bottle; kicking the grate with her heel to stir up wood char. Then she returned to the table and sat down, smoothing her middle-parted gray hair.

Thoughtful a moment, Mama then said, "All she knew was that the ship had wrecked. She'd seen her poor mother swept acrost the deck. Then a big wave got her an' her papa an' they tried to swim to the beach. An' that's all she remembered till you had her in the surf tonight. She didn't even know it had happened a month ago. Imagine that."

I asked, "You tell her that her mama and papa had gone loo'ard?"

Mama nodded. "I had to, Ben. She asked. I think she alriddy knew, up in the corners o' her mind. I couldn't tell her yes they was alive tonight an' no they was dead tomorrow. I said both had drownded. You heerd her sobbin' but she took it a lot better'n I expected. You wake up in a strange place an' have somebody tell you your folks are dead. Mercy!"

I nodded, relieved that I had not been in the room during that grim duty.

Mama let out a long sigh. "What is worse is that she has no one in England, not a livin' blood soul to go to. I did find that out. That lil' girl is purely alone. Lord knows what grief is up in her head an' what will come out bye 'n' bye. An' where does she go now? An' who to? That'll be things all o' us has to face on the morrow."

I looked off toward the room in which the Teetoncey girl slept. No wonder she couldn't find her tongue to talk much now. That girl, without sole kin, surely had a hard road to travel. I wondered what kind of orphan homes they had in London. Maybe workhouses after the age of eight.

"You ask her age?"

Mama replied, "She turned twelve a week before that ship come up out o' the Barbadoes, sailing from the port o' Bridgetown, a place Reuben has mentioned."

She was the same age as me. Yet she didn't look it. Being so small, she looked more nine or ten. Female ages are always tricky, I've found. Mama looked the same at fifty as those pictures of her at thirty-five—thin but noble and couthy, which means capable, with a nose as prominent as Bodie Island Lighthouse.

The kettle announced itself from the living room and Mama moved to it, speaking on the way. "While I was fixin' that Purple, I came to think I'd ask Filene to take his time callin' the assistant inspector who will undoubtedly call the British consul. Teetoncey needs some grace 'fore bein' hauled aroun' by officials, don't you agree?"

I nodded. Filene Midgett was our cousin, the keeper who commanded the U.S. Lifesaving Station at Heron Head. He had been involved with the wreck of the *Malta Empress.*

Mama poured the steaming water over the chopped and log-dried holly leaves for the cup of tea. We bought yaupon by the small bale though it was going out of fashion in favor of mainland tea in cans. "So long as no one's grievin' for her anywhere, it won't hurt to help her acrost her river o' sorrow. Least we can do, Ben."

Once again I nodded my agreement but sensed she had something else in mind. Far more.

"So you tell Filene in the mornin' not to hurry

hisself phonin' the assistant inspector nor that consul, a man that I don't like very much, at best. Knowin' how governmint works, they'll do nothin' but lay confusion out here an' Teetoncey don't need that now." Mama halted herself for an out-loud reminder. "I got to start rememberin' her proper name. Wendy! Wendy! Wendy!"

Mama fell silent a moment but had that planning look on her face, chewing her lower lip. "I jus' recollected somethin'. A week ago I ordered two gingham dresses from Chicago for Teetoncey but have let that letter sit. After you tell Filene in the mornin', you make the mail boat."

It would take six weeks to two months for that order to be filled, I well knew. "She's going to be around that long?"

Mama didn't answer directly. "Least we'll send her back to London lookin' respectable."

The few clothes she was wearing when she washed ashore in early November had been pretty much mommicked, torn up, in the surf and I had never found her other shoe. She was decked out in borrowed clothes and borrowed shoes, plus a dress Mama had made for her.

I gazed at the Widow O'Neal, as she was often known on the Banks, but did not speak my mind—Mama, why don't you plain admit you plan to keep that castaway girl awhile?

Instead and much safer, I said, "I'll go on to bed." That way, I might possibly get to sleep before she slipped in beside me and started to snore, which she could do with great power.

I did look in on the girl. She was having her sweet dreams. Her mouth was slightly open and her breathing was deep. That Purple medicine was not to be denied. Boo Dog had returned to the oval rug and lifted his big yellow head to stare at me as if I were an intruder. That fickle dog had taken it on himself to guard her, losing some noticeable respect for me.

I went on to bed but did not drop off right away. Mama stayed up for almost another hour, far past her eight o'clock bedtime unless it was a revival night in Hatteras village or up in Manteo. I'm sure she was thinking, too. Perhaps the good

Lord had decided to compensate her for the sea's killing of a good and righteous but unaffectionate husband, John O'Neal, and my second brother, Guthrie O'Neal. I am equally sure she had thought about it during the many previous days when the girl was ill of mind. Now that it was positively known that Teetoncey had no living soul to tend her, a purpose in the surf casting her up was clear. The good Lord had ordained it.

I heard Mama move out of the kitchen and into that small room where I'd lived since the crib. She was probably looking down on the Teetoncey girl again, probably fussing with the comforter for a moment; lowering the wick in the lamp so it couldn't possibly smoke.

I heard her whisper something to dumb old Boo Dog. Maybe, "Rout me if she wakes."

That woman certainly deserved a girl inasmuch as I hadn't turned out to be one. I had long lived with the painful fact that she'd hoped I'd be a female, then I wouldn't go to sea nor be a surfman and die in a gale. She'd even dressed me as a girl when I was five years old. I pretended I was fast asleep when she came in, and concentrated deeply on listening to the ocean roar.

A few miles away, to south and east, rows of high waves, cresting white in the blackness, rolled over Diamond Shoals, which lay off Cape Hatteras, and then raced toward the beach, finally passing under the warm beam of Hatteras Lighthouse. On north from Hatteras Point, they marched endlessly, going past Wimble Shoals and lesser bars to spend tons of water against our fragile but defiant Outer Banks.

Though the sand strips appeared to be slumbering for the night, entirely deserted, I knew there was movement on foot and mule and sand pony. Surfmen of the lifesaving stations were plodding along in the cold dampness above the grasping white water, now and then looking out to sea. During and after a gale of wind were the perilous times when the ships loomed suddenly, riding helplessly in spindrift that whipped off the long crests of Atlantic Ocean rollers.

I hoped that no ship would wreck that night yet it was always an exciting time when they did.

2

WHEN CALM DAYLIGHT widened over the beach
and sand ridges and flats, the sound-side marshes,
the scattered silvered houses and red-roofed surfmen stations, sharpening the whalebone fences
at some of the villages, word began to carry.
Soon, it would go from Nag's Head and Kill
Devil Hills on over to Roanoke Island, and then
down to Buxton Woods and Hatteras. I carried it
willingly.

Teetoncey could talk and knew who she was.

Long before she was awake, recuperating from

the events of the rough night, I rode Fid, our brown and white tackie, just an old, ugly big-hoofed sand pony, up to Heron Head Lifesaving Station and skidded off in back, by the cistern, near the door.

I opened it without formality and yelled in at Keeper Midgett, startling him.

"She's not crazy. Her name's Wendy Lynn Appleton, and she's from London."

Shoving back from the table and his swamped plate of pancakes and molasses, Filene said approvingly, "Well, I declare . . ."

Surfman Jabez Tillett, sitting opposite Filene, was caught with his mouth full and sputtered something no one could have detected.

Mark Jennette, another surfman, just in from patrol, said in astonishment, "Is that so?"

Lem O'Neal, third cousin of mine, and Malachi Gray were also eating.

They'd all thought the British girl was hopeless.

I took delight in repeating Mama's instructions. "Mama said don't call the inspector until you talk to her." I had changed it to make it a little more positive and saw Filene redden, as usual. There was always an undeclared war between Keeper Midgett and the Widow O'Neal, though they had admiration for each other. Yet I could never resist throwing on verbal coal oil.

I jumped back on Fid to depart the sturdy two-story government shingle that housed the surfmen and all their rescue equipment and life-saving boats. The building sat on dunes above the high-water mark, with a lookout cupola wedged in the juniper shingle roof.

Filene must have untangled his massive body from the table because he filled the doorway in a jiffy. He yelled, "How did it happen?"

Rapping both feet into Fid's shaggy belly, so he'd go to a fast trot, I yelled back, "Mama'll tell you. I got to make the mail boat, Cap'n."

As I drew away, Fid stretching out to a gallop, I heard Filene bellowing, in a voice loud enough to flatten the sea, "Ben O'Neal, come back here." Family cousin or not, I had long been petrified of that block-faced keeper, and conversations of any length tied my tongue and ended in untruthful webs. It was far better to pit Mama against him.

Besides, there was no doubt that Filene would soon board his own pony and trot inland to our house, there to confront Mama with her latest maneuver concerning that girl, absolutely unauthorized by the federal Lifesaving Service, which was law on the Outer Banks. There was also no doubt that Filene would lumber to the recently installed crank phone to ring all the stations— Nag's Head, Bodie Island, Oregon Inlet, Pea Island, New Inlet, Chicamacomico, Big Kinnakeet, Little Kinnakeet, Cape Hatteras. Filene would jubilantly pass the word and hint that he had some part of it: *Teetoncey, the castaway girl, had her brains unaddled.*

I understood his point of view more than Mama. Over a period of many shipwrecks, hundreds of them, nothing quite like it had ever happened on the Banks: The sole survivor of the *Malta Empress,* a snip of a girl of then indeterminate age, had been unable to utter a word, much to the chagrin of Filene Midgett, who prided himself on exacting accounts of wrecks. Regulations required precise survivors' reports and here was one who did not even mumble. Having logged seventy-one wrecks in his own time of heroic service, Filene could not remember such a patience-trying incident and often said so.

The outer sand trail, wide enough for a pony cart or mule wagon, running north and south just behind the dunes on the ocean side, was still wet from the night's nor'easter, stone gray except where wands of early sun touched here and there. There was another partial main track that followed close to the sounds—Currituck, Roanoke, Pamlico, etc.—on the west side of the Banks, connecting the villages. Then paths for foot or pony, crossing the Banks, extended to the sea between the two parallel trails, which sometimes blended.

There wasn't much on the beach itself, except the rotting-out hulks of wrecks every few miles, and plenty of driftwood which filtered off the Carolina mainland, washed out to sea through Oregon or Hatteras inlets, and then returned to the beach to soak up sun for a hundred years. Aside from the wrecks and hauling gill nets, stuck with sea trout or bluefish at sunset during spring, summer, and fall, the ocean sand didn't occupy us very much. Mainlanders sometimes sat on it or collected seashells, which was equally ridiculous. What can anyone do with a seashell?

I steered Fid, his nostrils steaming in the dawn cold, over a dune and dropped down to the beach just south of Heron Head Shoal, where the *Malta Empress* had broken up, and looked out at the white water churning over the bar. Mean water, always. Smooth as buttertop on a calm day, lapping innocently. Dangerous as a nest of cottonmouths when the blows come down from the north.

"We claimed her from you, all the way," I remember shouting defiantly toward the sandbar. I meant Teetoncey, of course. Might as well let the shoals know, too.

Then I cut sharp back inland and rode straight to Mr. Burrus's store at Chicamacomico village, *Chicky* village, a place of work for me several days a week, and jumped off on the flimsy porch, opening the door that had a brass bell from the wrecked schooner *Betty Coffyn* strapped to it.

Mr. Burrus looked around as I came jingling in. Thin sweater buttoned, overshoes and apron already on, felt hat perched low on his forehead, he was ready for the day and hopeful of doing more cash than credit business, an unusual circumstance. Our sand strips were poor, though not impoverished. There was plenty to eat. Gardens, cows, and pigs. Fish by the ton.

"Teetoncey talked," I had to blurt.

"I'll swan. You don't say. Well, I'll swan." Mr. Burrus, too, was truly surprised.

Mis' Burrus separated the burlap curtains that hid their living room from the front of the store. She was never too far from that curtain so as not to miss a juicy word. "She did talk, now?"

"Name's Wendy Lynn Appleton, and she's from London, like I told you I guessed long ago."

"That is a miracle," Mr. Burrus said soberly.

"She and her mama and papa boarded in the Barbadoes on their way to New York and London. That much we know. We hope she'll tell us more today . . ." My mouth got dry and I had to swallow. "Main thing, she knows who she is."

"Did it all by herself," Mr. Burrus wrongly concluded.

"Not at all," I was quick to say. "Mama sent me to the beach with her last night in the thick of that gale of wind. Hair of the dog that bites you! She come unloose at Heron Head, soon's she saw that wild water. Screaming and everything. I had a time with her. Whatever it was that got locked up in her mind because of the wreck got unlocked and she remembered it all, and got her speech back . . ."

I knew what Mis' Burrus would say next: "I do deceive the good Lord had a hand in this."

"Yessum," I answered respectfully, but I wondered where the good Lord had been hiding the night the *Empress* laid her splendid keel on the sand. That barkentine had been firewood in five minutes. Thirteen dead that the Lord didn't have to fret about again. I added pointedly, "But *He* also robbed her of every living soul she had. That girl is a convicted orphan now."

Mis' Burrus frowned at my notion that *He* had overstepped *His* bounds but Mr. Burrus only clucked sadly, rotating his round cheeks at Teetoncey's plight. He'd grown to like the girl, even when she couldn't talk.

A sallow man from the Post Office department, down from Elizabeth City, was in the store after having spent the night on a cot midst the cheese and dried apple smells. He asked what everyone was so excited about.

"Tell him, Ben," said Mr. Burrus.

I took a breath and retold it briefly, not that I minded. How the *Empress* had wrecked, and the sea had given up the girl, sprawling her icy on the beach to be found by Boo Dog and myself. How I'd carried her home and Mama nursed her back to life only to have Doc Meekins, with his noble book learning and in his whiskey breath, say she had a type of "catatonia," a shock of some kind. Now, she was cured.

Mis' Burrus, every bit as religious as my mama, added, like an amen, "Glory be!"

"You and your mama did a good turn," said

the eye-shaded man from the P.O. department, and kept on counting to make sure Mr. Burrus hadn't stolen any stamp money. There were no thieves on the Outer Banks and no door locks, but the government was always suspicious. To quote Jabez Tillett, "We are a damn sight more honest than any politician."

I bought a stamp in full view, licked it, pounded it on the Chicago letter, and then dropped it into the wire basket which was the total Post Office department at Chicky—wire basket so Mis' Burrus could easier snoop the addresses. The mail boat was still at the dock waiting for this beady-eyed man to finish his quarterly tabulations. There was no more business to transact in Chicky, and nothing more to say, so I departed.

Fid trotted south again along what was the narrowest point of the Banks, the stretch between Chicky and Clarks. There were a few houses in the hammocks south of Chicky; not enough to warrant them village status. The sand strips broaden out nearing Buxton Woods and Cape Hatteras, the widest part of the Banks.

The shallow Pamlico was still choppy from the dregs of the gale, mud-spoiled, and I couldn't see any boats out as yet. Not a sharpie, bugeye, or skiff anywhere. In the winter, especially in rough chop, no one was too anxious to check the fish nets, strung between poles, until the sun was nine o'clock high. Anything caught by the gills was safe until frost was off the boat seats. But the Pamlico could be treacherous any time of the year as my late brother Guthrie had discovered on a squally spring afternoon at the age of thirteen, manning a shad boat for Old Man Spencer.

Arriving home, I found Teetoncey was still asleep and I hadn't been there for more than two minutes when I looked out and saw Filene dismounting from his tackie that had no name beyond "hee" or "haw." A notebook was tucked beneath the keeper's arm and a stub of pencil was up behind his red right ear.

He tapped on the door and it was opened by Mama who said, "I was expectin' you, Cousin."

The surf captain tromped in, asking, "That girl awake?" He looked at me and just grunted, but then changed his mind. "Boy, when I call you, come back!" His eyes bored at me under bushy brows.

I said meekly, "Yessir." And meant it.

"No, she isn't awake, Filene," Mama said.

He frowned. "How long she been asleep?"

"'Bout twelve hours. I give her some Purple last night."

Filene said, "Can't you wake her up? That's enough sleep for anybody." He peered toward my room where he knew she'd been residing since early November. "She ain't sick, is she?"

Mama answered, "I don't intend her to be, an' I don't intend to wake her up. Come on in the kitchen where that bullfrog voice o' yours don't disturb her."

Filene took a deep, exasperated breath and followed Mama toward the kitchen. He was only trying to do his duty and get the wreck details. He had a responsibility to the Lifesaving Service.

I went as far as the door, reaching it at the point Mama said, "Write down your questions an' I'll have her answer 'em in her own good time."

Leaning up against the wooden sinkboard,

looking around for what might be cooking, rubbing a large thumb over a ripe persimmon, the keeper shook his close-cut head. He cut the top himself but let Jabez use an extra-large china bowl to get a straight neckline in the back. "I can't do that, Rachel," said Filene. A widower, with his children grown and gone, our cousin was more or less married to the surfboat station. "I cannot do it," he repeated.

"You might have to. I have no ideer what shape she's gonna be in when she wakes."

Filene studied Mama a minute and then his heavy jaw took a stronger set. "Ever since you got your hands on that girl, you have defied authority. Now, I'm tellin' you, Rachel O'Neal, she is the sole responsibility o' the Lifesavin' Service, an' now that we know for sure her citizenship, she is also a ward o' the British governmint. You have nothin' to say about her as o' this mornin'."

Mama was squinting. "Is that all?"

The keeper nodded.

I thought, Hang on to your tiller, Filene. You have no idea what this woman is planning.

Mama began quietly. "Allow me to say this, Cousin. We learned last night that when the great Lifesavin' Service didn't git to that ship in time, she lost her only livin' kin." Mama let that sink in and then added deftly, "She is twelve years ol' an' hasn't a solitary human to call her own."

Filene winced a bit. "I'm sorry to hear that." But he also quickly recovered from his sorrow. "You can't blame me for losin' her parents."

Mama answered softly and understandingly. "Havin' been a surfman's wife, I'd never place blame. But I do want to politely ask—did you call the assistant inspector in Norfolk?"

"I have those intentions when I git back to the station. This survivor can talk now. I cannot delay information of this importance. Inspector Timmons can then notify the consul."

Mama pleaded, "For her sake, don't call for a week." I suppose Mama figured that would give her time to entice Teetoncey to stay on.

The keeper shook his head. "I can't do that."

I saw Mama begin to harden when she used a

John Rollinson preachment on him: "A man o' words an' not deeds is like a garden o' weeds."

Filene had heard it many times. He repeated stubbornly, "I cannot do it."

Mama then poured lye into her next words. "Well, then I'm gonna ride to ever surf station on these Banks an' tell ever surf cap'n what an unfeeling jackass you are." Most people are more respectful to surf captains.

Filene clubbed the sinkboard with a heavy hand, causing a pot of soaking white beans to bounce. "Jackass, am I?" he exploded.

That woke the girl because we heard a startled cry from my room. In a fury, Mama chased the keeper out of the house. I hid my face so he couldn't see me laughing.

Later, I learned that he was so upset that he forgot to tell us that a brigantine, a small square-sailed ship, had wrecked off Bodie Island during the gale. Every man was saved by Keeper Filene Midgett and his crew.

3

AFTER THE DOOR slammed behind Filene, the girl came out of the room, a little wobbly legged and looking dazed. Purple could do that to you. Mama rushed over. I stayed back. During female crisis, whether it is a midwife problem or swampwater-juniper stains on a new dress, I do not think males are of much use.

Teetoncey stared at us as if we were total strangers, and I suppose we were, more or less.

Mama asked, very tenderly, "You feel better, child?"

She nodded, eyes scanning around the room as if she might have awakened in a feed bin. She blinked when she looked at Reuben's beautiful stuffed buck head on the west wall. Cletus Gillikin had done a lifelike job with the deer's eyes.

Later, I found out she'd also had quite a jolt waking up in my room, though she vaguely remembered it despite catatonia. Guthrie's Poteskeet arrowheads were wired to one wall; Reuben's *baleen*, which is filter for toothless whales, black, shiny, and curving, hairy fibers on one edge, was on another wall. My duck decoys were in one corner. Another corner had a big dried turtle shell sitting on a mullet throw net. For certainty, it was not like her own fancy room back in London. She could also smell seaboots and oakum boat caulking which I had never smelled in there before.

Though it was against my grain, I felt I had to say something. I asked, "How do you feel?"

She gazed at me with gray green eyes and answered mechanically, "Quite well, thank you."

Hah. If somebody had opened the door, the breeze would have knocked her over. But I did sense a weakening in the back of my own legs. I was not accustomed to a London voice and no one had ever thanked me for asking how they were. *Quite well, thank you.*

Mama said, "Ben, you go on about your business. We have to tidy up." That meant showing her to the outhouse, a chill trip in early December; changing from her wool nightshirt (one of mine) to a dress; some water on her face in the kitchen and a hair brushing. That routine had been staple for a month though Teetoncey hadn't been aware of it.

I had to split some wood, anyway, and went out back, keeping the seat of my pants in the direction of the outhouse, which was southwest of the woodpile.

A little later, when I filled the wood boxes in the front room, Mama was watching her brush her hair. Well, that was progress. A few minutes later, when I filled the wood box for the kitchen range, she was settled down at the table and ready to eat some cornbread with blackberry jam on it. There was pure cow milk—not goat milk—to go with it. Eggs, if she wanted them. Fried fatback for the asking. We ate well.

I said, "You feel better, huh?"

She nodded and smiled nervously. I'm still glad there was no sudden thunder or lightning cracks that forenoon. She would have gone up like a rocket.

I said, "You look better."

She smiled again. "Thank you."

I desperately wanted to talk about that wreck but thought it should wait awhile. She seemed too ginger as yet; still dazed and foggy in the head; viewing her new surroundings with all the courage of a lost doe.

Mama went on, "While we was hair brushin', I tol' her exactly where we lived. Between the ports o' Norfolk an' Charleston out on sand islands." Mama laughed happily. "She'll see 'em soon enough."

She'd already seen them but it hadn't mentally registered. I'd taken that girl from Hatteras

Lighthouse to the snow-geese grounds at Pea Island. There wasn't a thing she hadn't seen but was unknowing of it all.

I took another long look at her while she nibbled. Her daisy hair was neatly done and Mama had her in a long skirt and blouse, Lucy Scarborough's old shoes on her feet. There was some color back in her cheeks. She looked real fine.

Mama said, "I tol' her we'd probably be callin' her Teetoncey a lot since her true name is new to us."

Then this girl did a nice thing. She looked at Mama and said, "I understand."

That proved to me she was refined and had good manners. I had earlier suspected, from the labels on her dress and in one shoe, worn the night she was flung up on the beach, that she was also of means. No girl on the Banks had anything but a mail-order label on their dress collars. Of course, none of us knew much about rich people. Some came to Nag's Head in the summer to get away from *miasmi*, which is inland stinkery and germs. They seldom ventured this far south.

Mama then said to Teetoncey, "That man who so rudely woke you up is Filene Midgett, of some kin to us. He's been pesterin' us for weeks about that wreck, an' wanted to talk to you. But I run him out an' I doubt he'll be back for a day or so."

Having an interest in that possible discussion, I added, "He's a keeper with the Lifesaving Service. They have to make out wreck reports."

The girl glanced over. "I'll be glad to talk to him although it all happened very quickly." A shadow passed over her face and Mama changed the subject but not before tears began to stream down from Tee's eyes.

Mama gave me a sign with her head and I departed to go down to our little dock on the sound to work on my sailboat, *Me and the John O'Neal*. Just putter around.

That first day after Tee came out of her catatonic state was vexing for everyone. Coming into a strange place, with strange faces, knowing her folks were dead, it's a wonder she didn't crawl back into her head and never come out again.

A little later, Mama walked down to the dock

and said, "Go over to Mis' Scarborough an' ask her to git word to all the women that we're not to home for twenty-four hours. No visitin'. Especially Hazel Burrus." That was wise.

"How is she?" I asked.

"Poor thing. She's either weepin' or jus' starin'."

As I went to the shed to get Fid's bridle, Mama called after me. "Keep Kilbie an' Frank away, too." They were my best friends and never off-limits. Harboring a castaway has its penalty.

I nodded.

Supper that night was not much better and Teetoncey had no more words than a baked duck, which is what we had to eat. But Mama went on, as usual. Tee fled the table midway and sprawled out on the bed, Mama following her close. I went on eating, unable to assist. The last I saw of Tee before I went to bed, she was on her belly on the rag rug, stroking Boo Dog, who was getting more enjoyment out of this than anybody.

Morning broke and somehow Teetoncey had

put her boat in order. Maybe she'd had time to think during the night and realize that we might be humble folks but we meant well. Besides, she didn't have much choice. She was kinless. Anyway, she was almost human in the morning, almost cheerful, talking a little bit instead of crying and moping. Right off, she talked strangely, calling a dress a frock.

My chores of chopping wood and emptying the garbage pail and filling the oil lamps were done about eight-thirty, almost the same time that Teetoncey finished helping in the kitchen—she'd volunteered, to my amazement—and I raised the window to ask, "You like to ride Fid?"

"Oh, very much," Tee responded.

Mama cautioned her. "Sometimes that pony can act up."

"I'll be quite all right, thank you," the girl answered, as British as ever.

Before I could get five feet away, I heard Mama stealthily warn her, "Ben might not be like boys in your country. He's rough at times." That made me mad.

"I'll watch myself, Mrs. O'Neal," was her reply.

Then Mama came to the window and looked out at me, didn't say a word but gave me cold eyes—Ben, you hurt her and I'll have Filene strop your mooney.

I returned her look with as much innocence as possible, then got Fid and brought him up about the time Tee came off the stoop in one of my old sweaters. The red bob-cap Mr. Burrus had contributed to her wardrobe was on her head.

I said, "Teetoncey, I'll help you up on him, then take the reins . . ."

"I think I can get up," she said, and with that, she went up backward, a kind of hike, like she had springs in her toes. I was surprised.

Fid was low to the ground but I still had to jump up a little to board him. I wondered why and how she'd done it but didn't ask. "Now, swing a leg over him."

She looked at me calmly. "If you don't mind, I prefer to ride this way."

"With both legs on one side. You got no saddle."

She nodded and grasped the reins with one hand, Fid's mane with the other.

It seemed to me that she was just showing off like a circus rider and I did something without really thinking about it. Yet I suppose it had been in the back of my mind. She'd annoyed me off and on—taking over my room, sleeping in my bed, practically stealing Boo Dog from me. I shrugged and looked back to see if Mama was watching. She was nowhere to be seen. Just to get him started, I drew back and hit Fid on the rump hard enough to stun my wrist-bone. I didn't mean to whack him that hard.

He shot out, and I fully expected to see Tee dump. But she stayed on at least forty feet down the path until she pitched into a myrtle bush.

I walked on down to help her out. Her face was red and I couldn't tell whether she was hurt or angry, but her eyes had some fire in them. At least, she wasn't thinking about her dead folks.

I said, "You'll learn."

Fid was about twenty feet away, gnawing on clump grass, and she went over to him, took the reins, did the odd backward spring, grabbed his mane, and clucked him away. She called back to me in a cool, crisp tone. "I ride sidesaddle in England, Ben. I'm really very good at it."

I stood there a long time, watching the red bob-cap go up and down through the low dunes. It occurred to me that she might have some spunk. It also occurred to me that if she ever fell off into any of our prickly pear or Spanish dagger she might "prefer" to ride the way we did, nestling the animal.

In early afternoon, I took Tee over to see Filene at Heron Head Station. Mama begged off because she was not up to wrangling with Filene so soon again but instructed me to withdraw Teetoncey if she got tired from all the questions.

We bumped and wound east in the pony cart along the trail to Filene's station. Boo Dog trotted behind, keeping his sympathetic black eyes pinned on Teetoncey. Some ruddy ducks angled across the clear blue winter sky, leaving sharp cries in their wake. Boo didn't even look up, having been taken captive by a female. In fact, I think he'd convinced himself that he alone had found and saved this girl. Miserable hound.

Holding on, looking around, Teetoncey said, "I have never seen such desolate land." Compared to London, I suppose it was.

Like white-gray meringue, windblown sand ridged up here and there, sparsely dotted with clumps of spiked grass. Now and then, roots of sea-tumbled stumps, sent in on raging tides, reached out like dark witches' fingers. Toward the ocean there was not so much as a shack to break the bleak landscape. I had read something of London and this did not resemble the palace grounds or that place that sounded like a jar of relish, Piccadilly.

"Have you always lived out here?" she asked.

I nodded.

"Does everyone fish for a living?"

"That and lifesave," I said. "But not me, personally. Mama does not take to me going out on the water. I do store work. Otherwise, I suppose I'd be fishing, at least." The sounds were good for that, and shad was the best money fish.

There had been sturgeon around, but they were gone now. There was always mullet but mainlanders hadn't really learned how to eat them.

"Your mother told me that you'd seen what was left of the *Malta Empress*."

I glanced over. "Both that night and the next day."

"What did you see?"

"Timbers busted up. Some clothes, boots. Barrels. Anything that would float. Spars." I decided not to discuss the row of bodies under the tarpaulins, nor to say I'd seen her papa after Jabez dropped him, mouth open and stony dead, at Filene's feet that night. "There wasn't much to see."

"No chests?"

Now, that was a very odd thing she wanted to know about. I shook my head. "I didn't see any. They don't float unless there's a lot of air space in them. Truly, there wasn't enough of that ship for the wreck commissioner to come down. Not enough for *vendue*. That's auction. Everybody bids on what is left."

She was thoughtful for a minute. "Where did it happen?"

"Not far from here. About two miles. I'll show you someday." Of course, she'd seen it two nights ago; once before that in daylight. I had to keep reminding myself of that blank period in her life.

We were just about to the ocean and I drove the cart up on a dune. The ridge sloped down to the beach and tideline. "Stand up, Teetoncey," I said, "and you'll see a sight most people have never seen."

Planting her feet in the canvas bag behind Fid's tail, she rose up and saw our skeletons of ships that stretched for miles along the beach in both directions. She didn't say much for a moment but then asked, "Did the *Empress* look like that?" She pointed to the nearby *Hettie Carmichael,* which had most of her keel, a lot of ribbing, and some of her stern left.

I said, "Not at all. What was left of the *Empress* could be put in five mule wagons." I did not tell her the Gillikins were having an extra room built from timbers of the *Empress.*

We went on to Heron Head Station with Tee in a pond of silence.

Although he gave me a dark look, Keeper Midgett was most kind to Teetoncey. He introduced her to all the surfmen, as if they'd never seen her before. They made over her, especially Jabez. Then Filene found a bottle of sarsaparilla but she declined it and true to himself, he didn't offer me any. Finally, he got his notebook with smudged pages on it, showing signs he'd thumbed it a hundred times; then that stub of pencil began moving jerkily across paper as if it had a brake on, swallowed in his thick fingers.

Surprisingly, she didn't tell us much more than we already knew. But it was of intense knowledge to learn that the bark had blown its sails out one day past Norfolk, then drifted back, rudder shackled, at the mercy of the long rollers, until it foundered on Heron Head Shoal. Her papa had tried to swim to the beach, as Jabez had guessed, after her mama had been bashed on deck. We also learned that her papa, who was a landholder and a barrister, which is like a lawyer, had chartered that ship, paid fully for her voyage from New York to the Barbadoes and back. That took a pretty penny, I was guessing. So the Appletons had to be rich. There were some other details that would not be of interest to land-faring people—a sea flooded her steam boiler for the donkey engine, stopping the pumps.

Speaking very officially, Filene said, "Of the thirteen bodies, we identified what we thought was your mama and papa. There was also a man I took to be the master by the way he was dressed . . ."

Teetoncey said, "His name was Hawkins."

Filene slowly wrote it down.

"There was also a peg-legged man."

Tee said, "The only name anyone called him was Ezra. He was the cook. A West Indian."

Filene wrote it down and then asked, "Miss, did you happen to see the cargo manifest o' that ship? What was aboard her? I git the impression she was in ballast." Ballast was mainly empty but with enough rock aboard to keep her steady.

Naturally, not being a sailor, Tee asked, "What is a manifest?"

"A list o' cargo an' passengers. We found a pad

of 'em off the *Empress* but they were blank. Didn't tell us anything but the ship's name." He dug around in a drawer of his rolltop desk and came up with some old water-stained manifests off other ships. He adjusted his specs on his nose for close reading and then said, "Somethin' like this." He began to toll them off: "Schooner *Donald Beam*, master-owner Hugh Beam, out o' St. Thomas, thirty tons o' ballast, nine hundred oranges, barrel o' yams, one demijohn gin, one thousand dollars in gold . . ."

I looked at Teetoncey. Her eyes had narrowed. I wondered why.

"Here's another one," said Filene. "Brigantine *Herbert Pettit*, master Craig Thompson, thirty-four puncheons o' molasses, eleven barrels o' sugar, one bundle o' letters, twelve hundred bushels o' salt, seven hundred fifty dollars in gold . . ."

Teetoncey shook her head, saying, "I did not see anything like that." But she had a queer look on her face, as if a small goose egg might be stuck in her throat.

Filene said, "Well, she mus' 'ave been in ballast. We didn't see any signs o' cargo."

Tee fell silent once again.

Filene stood up. "Bye 'n' bye, we'll hear from the Barbadoes an' from Lloyds o' London."

I came out of my refuge in the corner, where I'd been listening, but Filene said loudly, "I haven't finished, Ben . . ."

I retreated.

To Teetoncey he said gently, "We took the normal respects with those bodies, Mark Jennette carved an *A* on the crosses we thought was your mama and papa."

"Thank you," said Tee, visibly sad.

Then Filene eyed me sharply. "Tell your mama I did not eat this girl alive."

I nodded respectfully and took Teetoncey up to the lookout cupola where Luther Gaskins was on duty, watching a three-masted schooner through the long glass. Then I showed her the equipment room with the breeches buoy, which is like a pair of sawed-off canvas pants, hanging under a round ring float which resembles a mainland toilet seat. The canvas pants run on a line between the wrecked ship and shore. I also showed her the lifesaving car, which is shaped like a cigar and holds four men; dangles beneath the line from shore to ship; next, the lap-boarded surfboats which were rowed out to wrecked vessels. She was impressed. She also liked the practice wreck pole and I took pains to say I'd once had a wild ride down from it in a breeches buoy.

But a Hatteras cat had her tongue all the way home. She was clearly troubled about something above and beyond her deceased folks.

When we got to the house I found out that the mail rider had brought a letter from Reuben. He said he was sorry but he'd be gone on the *Elnora Langhans* for at least another eight months. The coasting brig was now shuttling cargo between Port Fernandino and Trinidad. He sent us a hundred dollars which was plenty to last between now and spring, when Mama and I would start making gill nets again, especially since I was still getting five dollars a month from the Burrus store. Mama was sad, though, that Reuben would be gone so many months. I missed him, too.

4

TEETONCEY WAS a chatterbox at supper and I suppose it was because she was still bereaved and frightened; still uneasy in a strange house and unknowing of us, though that was changing. Mama said that people who are skitterish sometimes talk a lot and say nothing. She said plenty. Whatever was priming her pump, it all gushed out. That girl evidently knew her London.

I learned that Teetoncey lived in a fancy section called Belgravia, off Belgrave Square, near Hyde Park, in a four-story house that had iron-railed balconies. I had guessed, previously, that she lived in a fancy place so Belgravia was not a surprise. They had a horse tender, known as a groom, and a gardener and a gardener's boy, and a parlormaid and a housemaid and "tweeny" maids, which I took to be maids that ran between the floors. They also had a house in the country and Teetoncey went to a private school. Sundays, in season, they strolled in Hyde Park with her papa in a top hat and her mama with an umbrella, even though it wasn't raining. My mouth was open the whole time as was the mouth of Widow O'Neal.

I left when Mama started talking about having a "tea" so that all the women on the Outer Banks could hear about London firsthand. I wondered where Mama herself had heard about teas, but it didn't matter. My head swimming with knowledge of Queen Victoria, London Bridge, trains of the Great Northern Railroad where you could eat in a padded chair, horse buses with seats on the roof, I went over to Kilbie Oden's house, a few hammocks up from us.

Kilbie was in the kitchen, honing fish knives

for his papa. Frank Scarborough was there, too. Without his white speckling of niter salve that night, Kilbie's pimples were worse than usual. His red hair wasn't combed. From his neck up, he seemed to be flaming. But out of all the pimples and brick hair came light blue eyes. Kilbie was a startling-looking boy.

I began to tell them everything that had happened the last two days, but Frank Scarborough, who was as handsome as Kilbie was uncomely, said, "We alriddy heerd." Then I started to tell about London, via Teetoncey, but they weren't interested in that, either.

Zipping a thin blade back and forth over the hone stone, Kilbie looked up with those stabbing blue eyes. "She ain't gonna be with you long, Ben."

"How do you know that?" I asked.

"Filene got word 'bout suppertime from Inspector Timmons that the British consul would leave Norfolk tomorrow an' come out an' pick her up."

"Who said?"

Frank opened his mouth. "Luther Gaskins tol' Papa."

"Why hasn't Filene tol' Mama?" I asked.

Kilbie thought he knew. "He's feared o' tellin' her, plenty some. He didn't think it'd go this fast. Filene knows your mama is attached to that girl, an' he's lickin' his lips tryin' to think o' a way to tell her."

There went a lot of plans. Earlier in the day I had been thinking of using that girl to ease me out of the house. I was already out of my own room and bed, and with her around to jabber about dresses and things there wouldn't be such a ruckus when I went to Norfolk and started asking at the ship chandlers for a cabin boy's berth. No one could accuse me of abandoning Mama if Teetoncey settled in. I said, "The consul can't do that."

Frank said, "You don't own her." That was true.

I left Kilbie's house with half a mind to go to Heron Head Station and confront Keeper Midgett but thoughts of such a meeting raised a ticking in my stomach. So I took a long time walking home under the stars, trying to figure out what we might do. The route I followed avoided the beach because all the ghosts of drowned sailors stagger around there at night, a truth and not a rumor.

What was a certainty was the arrival of the consul in three or four days. Say he'd take the train to New Bern or Elizabeth City, on the mainland, he'd then get aboard either the white steamers *Newbern* or *Neuse* and dock at Skyco, on the west side of Roanoke Island; then somebody would pick him up in a Creef, a sharp-prowed shad boat, and sail him on down here. The steamers made a mail, iced-fish, and passenger stop at Skyco in early morning or late evening. But the whole trip from Norfolk, train included, wasn't more than two or three days. There was precious little time.

It seemed to me there was only one thing to do—*hide Teetoncey.* Kidnap her, if she was willing.

If the British consul, a miserable man named Henry Calderham, Esquire, could not find her, he could not spirit her away to England. On the other hand, it occurred to me that Teetoncey might not want to be hidden on the Outer Banks; she might even want to go back to London. On second thought, had it been me I would welcome the consul, as foul a man as he was. I would welcome any man, woman, or child who got me off the Banks.

Reaching home about ten, I decided not to inform Mama. Maybe Filene would come over in the morning with the bad news. Slipping in beside her, I barely listened while she jabbered on in a low voice about other things the girl had said while I was gone. Of some interest was the fact that Tee had crossed the ocean in an iron steamship named *Lucania* in less than six days. But that information was not of much interest in view of our new predicament. I put the *Lucania* out of my head to think about a way to persuade Teetoncey to stay; then hide her. I could sail her over to the mainland and hang around east of Alligator River. Or we could hole up on Hog Island, which is east of the Mattamuskeet shore. There was no problem to hiding her.

Just before we went to sleep, Mama said that Tee wanted to see the graves where Filene had buried her folks. That was not a problem, either.

In the morning, I hitched Fid to the pony cart while Mama fretted that we had no fresh flowers to put on the graves. After the first frost, there is not a decent-looking unbrowned flower on the Banks except in Buxton Woods, closer to the Gulf Stream, and that was too far to go on short notice. So Mama finally got the idea to cut two cloth roses off an old black hat of hers, which she did.

Still harboring my knowledge of what was going to occur in a few days when Consul Calderham arrived, I rode in the back of the cart with that fickle gold hound while Mama and Tee sat on the seat. Mama, handling the reins, told Tee her parents should feel at home on the Banks since most of us had British blood, from castaways of past shipwrecks. Our grandparents settled down and stayed.

The Hatteras graveyards are all on high ground, back toward the sound shore. Even so, storms occasionally push the tide into the grave-yards, sometimes causing unpleasant tasks when the water drains away. The foremost graveyard is well behind candy-striped Hatteras Lighthouse but Filene had selected the burying ground near Chicky for the victims of the *Malta Empress*.

Teetoncey wept a little when looking at the crosses on which Mark Jennette had carved *A* for Appleton, especially when Mama handed over two cloth roses to pay respects. I'm thankful it was not gray and grim out there. The sun was up strong and the land looked cheerful. A few hardy birds chittered in the gnarled oaks nearby. It was even warm.

They dropped me off at the Burrus' store and went straight on home, since Tee was feeling tender. It was most fortunate that they did not stop to visit Hazel Burrus. Right off, Mis' Burrus said to me, "We heerd the British consul is comin' out to git Teetoncey." The news had traveled to everywhere except the O'Neal house. As I worked throughout the morning and after-noon, various people commented on it, saying it was a shame for the Widow O'Neal to lose her treasured girl so soon. I agreed, for different reasons, but did not mention them. If Tee stayed on, I'd have a chance to bid fare thee well to the Banks.

I finished about four o'clock and walked on to the house, deciding it was absolute time to tell Mama if she didn't already know. They were sitting on the stoop when I arrived, all dressed up as if it were Easter afternoon. Teetoncey smiled prettily and said, "Hello, Ben."

"Howdy," I answered, taking a closer look at them. They were wearing shawls over their blouses.

It was hard to believe. Except for weddings and funerals, Mama never got this dressed up on a weekday. She'd put an Italian brooch, one Reuben had traded off with a German sailor down in Porto Rico, at the throat of her blouse. She was even wearing those extra-high button shoes that hurt her feet. Neither of them looked down in the dumps from having been informed that Henry Calderham, Esq., was on his way.

Speaking almost snooty, Mama said, "Ben, we'll have dinner at five-thirty. You best git washed up." (I did have some dried blood on my hands from killing and plucking a hen for Mis' Burrus. Now that I noticed it, there were a few chicken feathers stuck to my trousers.) Then it dawned on me what Mama had said. *Dinner*. We always ate dinner at noon; supper at night.

Puzzled, I went past them into the house and saw that Mama had set up the small, square, oak living-room table on which usually sat the lamp over a doily. There were three chairs at the table. Except for holidays, for years we'd been eating in the kitchen on red-checked oilcloth. Old linen napkins from the wreck of the *Colleen Deviny* had come out of the trunk and were by the tin cups. There was even a candle, stuck in an Arab silver holder from Grandpa Cap'n Isaac O'Neal's inheritance, in the middle of the table. No one could have believed what was going on in the front room under the soulful stare of Reuben's buck.

Mama followed me into the kitchen where I went to wash up. Her eyes sparkling, she said happily, "I want Teetoncey to know we have some manners out here. You change into your best knickers, an' put a tie on, Ben. We'll eat proper."

I looked at her in amazement. She did seem ten years younger this late afternoon. I'm sure she brushed the gray strands of her hair for an hour. The bun at the back of her neck had never been so precise. There wasn't a speck of grime under her blunt fingernails. She'd also put some powder on her long nose so it couldn't possibly shine.

This was what a girl around the house could cause, I thought. The Widow O'Neal was finally happy and I didn't have the heart to tell her, just then, about the visitor from Norfolk. Maybe he'd get gout and couldn't disembark from the *Neuse*.

But I must say I enjoyed eating by candlelight, with Mama chewing slowly and talking softly, putting on airs for the first time since I'd known her. I also enjoyed watching Teetoncey eat. Daintily, she was doing something with her fork and knife and black-eyed peas. I had always used a knife to cut with but she was using it to eat with, helping load peas to the fork. She'd smile when she'd catch me looking at her.

To think I'd first discovered this same girl sprawled on the beach half dead; battered and bruised from the surf, skin whitish blue. Now, she sat wholesome and alive, with high cheekbones and good straight teeth, nose a little sharper than most. I'd have to admit she was prettier than any of the Banks girls. None had that yellow daisy hair. I was beginning to have dangerous mixed feelings, varying from hour to hour, about Tee. Liking her one day; disliking her the next.

"What kind of meat is this?" she asked. "It's very good."

"Wild pig roast," Mama answered. Then she looked over at me. "Jabez sneaked it out o' Heron Head mess this mornin'. Good thing Filene didn't catch him."

Filene had more to worry about than wild pig, I thought. I said, "Yes," anyway.

Teetoncey ate delicately, unlike the Gillikin girls. "This bread is delicious, what is it?" she asked politely, after a bird bite of it.

Mama said, "You fleech me, Wendy. It's spoon-bread. I'm proud that you like it."

The girl smiled graciously and said, "I do. And I also like living here. Already. And, you know, I'd really rather have you call me Teetoncey. It's such a lovely name."

Mama practically melted and I thought, *Oh, boy, you two had better hang on to your straps.*

As an afterthought, the girl asked, "What does 'fleech' mean?"

"Means to flatter," I answered. I'd already told her but she hadn't remembered.

Mama said, "I do think you'll enjoy stayin' out here with us for a while. Ben can show you eighty-foot whale skeletons an' take you up in the lighthouses."

"Oh, that's ripping," the girl replied excitedly.

Yes, a big rip *is* due, I thought.

Then they got to talking about the future and Mama said she just couldn't wait until the mail boat brought those new dresses from Chicago and Teetoncey said she'd like to embroider something for the house. She'd learned how in London. They bubbled on for ten minutes about happy times to come and then I thought I'd have to do it. I cleared my throat and said, "Mama, the British consul has left Norfolk to come out and get Teetoncey."

The girl dropped her fork and Mama rose half out of the chair. Her face turned the color of used soapsuds. She said, "Ben, don't jest me."

"I'm not jesting, Mama. Filene called the assistant inspector and he called the consul."

Mama left the table to look out the window toward Heron Head Station. I could almost feel her anger rising.

Teetoncey started to cry. "I don't want to go," she shrieked.

Mama came back from the window and said, "You don't have to go, child." She put her arms around the girl.

The girl actually wanted to stay.

5

EVEN BEFORE BREAKFAST, Mama, restless and churning all night, said, "There's only one thing to do, Ben. Hide her! Hide her good till that British consul leaves."

So, you see, I did not have to advance the scheme myself. However, being of the same mind, I grinned triumphantly. "There are plenty of places," I said, knowing more of them than she did.

Mama nodded with determination as she put the coffee on and laid some fatback in the skillet.

Then when Tee came into the kitchen to wash up after her trip to the outhouse, I announced, "We're going to hide you."

Her thin face beamed. "Yes, yes," she said, clapping her hands in a female fashion. "When will we do it?"

"A night or two," Mama said, with firmness. "Now, I know it is against the law to do this, Teetoncey, but takin' you away to let that consul declare your fate is against everthin' human and Christian. The British governmint can wait awhile."

The issue was thereupon decided on the grounds of humanity and Christians.

I immediately suggested taking Tee over to Hog Island, which was between Long Point and Bluff Point, off the mainland shore of the Pamlico. It was inhabited only by birds and fiddler crabs. Some fishermen had put a shack up on it long ago. With a few boards tacked up, it could be livable for a month. But Mama voted that down, not wanting us to cross the sound in my sailboat. Though she didn't mention the incident,

I had dumped the boat the previous month, almost drowning.

I then suggested hiding Tee in one of the windmills. There was enough space inside the small shingled housing to live for a while, though it might be drafty. The mills, up on stilts, were in disuse, and the sails, which are the turning vanes, hadn't been grinding corn for several years. Nobody ever came near them except for stray mainlanders who thought they were quaint.

"No," Mama said thoughtfully, "we'll find a place to hide her in warmth, with decent food an' a good bed."

To me, that was very dangerous. There were so many loose tongues on the Banks and Filene would go door-to-door asking for Teetoncey. Since nobody wanted to be caught with a goose egg passing their Adam's apple, they would not lie about it. The result would be that Henry Calderham would spirit her away.

We talked it over all through breakfast with no solution. Mama did say, "We should see our cousin this morning. If he gits the notion we plan to play the fox, he'll camp here."

I hadn't thought about that.

After chores, we went to Heron Head Station and on the way Mama said to Teetoncey, "Now, you jus' tell Filene Midgett you'll do what is right, an' let the rest to me. I'm not askin' you to tell a lie. In this case, doin' what is right is stayin' away from the consul."

Teetoncey nodded but I also noticed she swallowed. Like myself, I don't think she was looking forward to that face chopped out of quarry rock. Under those bushy brows, Filene's eyes could rivet through an anvil, or so it seemed. But if he expected Mama to blow him out of the water, he was mistaken.

As we entered, Mama said pleasantly, "Why, g'mornin', Cousin."

Filene was prepared for the worst. He took a nervous breath and said, "Mornin', Rachel." Then he greeted Tee and me but acted like he hoped Mark Jennette would call him up to the cupola for an emergency.

Mama said, "I heerd a rumor that the British consul is comin'."

Still narrow-eyed and wary, Filene said, "That's right, Rachel. I'm expectin' him tomorry."

Mama said forthrightly, "I'll pack what few clothes Teetoncey has an' git her ready."

Filene didn't know what to say. "Well, Rachel, I, ah . . . thought . . . ah . . ."

"I know what you thought," Mama broke in. "I'd come over here an' act like an aggravatin' woman."

Filene laughed. "I did. I sure did." He was much relieved.

Mama said quietly, "We'll do what's right."

The keeper peered over at Teetoncey. "And how about you, Miss?"

"Whatever is right, sir," she answered, so mannerly.

Filene laughed again. "Well, I never." He shook his head. "Consul Calderham will be surprised."

"That he will," Mama agreed. "When did you say he was comin'?"

"Tomorry. I'm sendin' Jabez up to Skyco today to git him. He'll be on the steamer. Then I suspect they'll leave here the next day. The consul is not taken with the Banks, as you know."

Mama said, "I hope he has a pleasant voyage," and then beckoned us out of the station.

Filene smiled and waved from the door, likely unable to believe he'd steered a shallow channel over the Widow O'Neal without once scraping bottom.

Hearing what Mama had said about a pleasant voyage, I had an idea. "I'll walk home," I said. "I want to see Jabez."

Jabez was sitting out in the sun on the north side of the station, splicing some manila line that he'd laid over a thimble. "How do, Ben," he said.

I squatted in the sand very near him so I could talk low. "I hear you're going to get that consul soon."

Jabez nodded unhappily. "I'll leave after noon chow. Truly, I was hopin', for your mama's sake, that he wouldn't come out for a month or so."

I said, "Jabez, you had great respect for my papa, didn't you?"

68

"I sure did," he answered.

"You like Mama and me, don't you?"

"I sure do."

I lowered my voice even more. "An' you saw how that consul acted when he was here before. He was unfeeling toward that girl."

"Yep."

"Well," I said, "we'd consider it a family favor if you'd make sure the consul has a rough trip out."

Jabez spit a gob of tobacco saliva about eight feet, and then sniffed. He knew what I meant.

There are ways of sailing a boat that are uncomfortable. You take some waves bow-on, and the cold water sloshes into the boat. You don't quarter them but plow in. When you come around on a tack, you let her pound a little more; wallow some. You might even get very sloppy when you come around and let the boom hit the passenger in the head. All it takes is a mite of pressure with your elbow on the tiller and a keen eye to the wind and waves.

Jabez grinned suddenly. "Well, Ben, if there's fifteen or twenty knots o' wind, even ten, I jus' don't see how it won't be a rough trip in an open boat, an' I'll make sure I got one. In mid-December, these sounds can be as mean as treed polecats, I tell you."

I got up. "Appreciate it, Jabez."

Chinless Jabez, built like a long bean, chuckled and took another spit and pulled his splice tight.

I went home.

About noontime, I was not really surprised when Mama got me aside to say, "Ben, you'll have to hide her an' not tell me where she is. Filene'll ask an' I've got to be able to say I jus' don't know. She's gone visitin', that's all. But don't you take her out on the water. Keep her in a warm place an' feed her."

I had been thinking about just such a place and a little later got aboard Fid, who was having a workout these days, and trotted south. Reaching the area of Buxton Woods, I left the trail so I could come up in back of Mis' Creedy's house and not be seen. I tied Fid down in the marsh and walked the last half mile to her cottage, which was surrounded with clematis, with its apple-green flowers, and red myrtle; wisteria clumped over her south porch in season. There was some deerberry not far away. It was a pretty setting.

A nice fire crackled on her iron firedogs, which I had always admired, and Mis' Creedy didn't seem to be doing much of anything but sitting near the heat in a comfortable chair. A thick book was on the arm, and I made a guess she'd been reading. As a former schoolteacher in Iredell County, left with an inheritance, and now a bird painter, she had no schedule to meet other than cooking for herself. People had tried to match her off, but a plump, white-haired woman of sixty, set in her ways, is not easy to match. Besides, she was a mainlander, born in Blowing Rock, which was in the mountains. I reminded myself to tell Teetoncey not to be startled when she saw Mis' Creedy in men's pants. She was the only woman on the Banks who wore them, tucked into regular seaboots. They protected her legs when she was painting waterfowl.

It took a few minutes for me to explain exactly

what was happening and Mis' Creedy accepted it with a mixture of nods and frowns. When I finished, she said, "Hmh," got up and walked over to one of her heron paintings on an easel, scanned it, rubbed her double chin, rearranged some dried wild coffee, which is a delicate fern, and came back to sit down.

"Ben, I don't know," she said, plainly worried.

"It'll only be a few days. Maybe a week," I said. "You two can talk about London." Mis' Creedy was the only one on the Banks who'd ever been to London.

She was still troubled. "I'd like to have her stay with me, Ben. Sometimes it's lonely here. But have you and your mother really thought this out? She's a citizen of another country, and the consul represents that country. I think you're breaking the law."

Then I told Mis' Creedy how the consul acted just after the *Empress* wrecked, badgering the girl because she couldn't talk.

"How does Teetoncey feel about it?"

"She wants to stay awhile," I said. "She doesn't have a soul in England to go to."

Mis' Creedy sat and thought a moment more, and then laughed merrily, slapping her ample knee. "All right," she said. "It's about time I do something exciting. Bring her down. I suppose we have to keep it a big secret."

"Yes, we do," I said, thinking of all the snooping that went on from Nag's Head south. "I'll bring her tomorrow night."

Mis' Creedy laughed again. "Ben, you do get yourself involved in things."

That was correct. Having been born on the dark of the moon, on an incoming tide, a hooty owl seen by the midwife to be perched in our pathway scrub oak, it was ordained that many strange things would happen to me.

Early the next night, Mama kept Boo Dog in the house so he wouldn't follow us, and then, under stars, we ambled toward Buxton Woods in the pony cart, with Tee chattering away. She was all wound up and looking forward to staying with Mis' Creedy. I listened but was more interested in the waves on the sound and the strength of the wind, knowing that Jabez was scudding down the Pamlico with Consul Calderham. I prayed that the small sharpie boat, borrowed from Cletus Gillikin, was pitching and pounding and taking on water.

A half-wild sheep appeared suddenly in the trail and that startled Tee for a moment. But the animal just plunged off into the brush and the trip was uneventful.

After settling Tee in at Mis' Creedy's, I returned to Chicky village to wait for Jabez and the consul. It was then about ten o'clock and my dead-reckoning estimate, with a fifteen-knot breeze, would put Jabez up to the Chicky dock about eleven. I knocked on the Burruses' back door to borrow a lantern and then went to the dock to wait. That breeze certainly had a cold edge on it.

Sure enough, about ten to eleven, I sighted the sharpie sail coming out of blackness and then Jabez brought the boat smartly up to the dock, dropping his canvas perfectly. I caught his line and wove it on a cleat, then looked into the boat for Consul Calderham. He was hunched on a seat. Jabez tapped him on the shoulder and then helped him out, saying to me, "Oh, it was cold 'n' wet out there tonight."

"Is that right, Jabez?" I answered, acting very surprised.

The consul stood on the dock like he was benumbed and I looked at him in the lantern glow. The roof of his derby hat appeared to have frost on it, and he was soaked from his muskrat collar to his feet. His teeth were clicking and a *zissssss* sound was coming from his blue lips. He was in terrible condition and I ran back to the Burrus store to borrow a blanket.

Eventually, we helped Mr. Calderham into the pony cart and I drove them to Heron Head Station, where we practically lifted the consul out and helped him into the warmth, where Filene was waiting.

The keeper took one look at the wet, frozen consul and was puzzled. So Jabez said quickly, "Cap'n, it was real rough out there tonight. I took more water aboard than usual."

Filene's eyes narrowed, so I left.

6

FILENE came over midmorning to collect Tee-toncey.

Mama asked, "How's the consul?"

"Not good," Filene replied. "He's got a terrible cold, Rachel. I could swear there wasn't that much wind yestiddy. Jabez can take a boat down the sound in a gale without loosenin' a peg, yet he must'a half swamped last night. The consul looked like he'd been underwater half the time."

"You need a penetrate for him?" Mama asked.

"No, I doctored him good but he is ill today,"

said the keeper. "Despite that, he wants to go. But he refuses to take a boat again. I'll pass him up the line overland, station to station, an' the boys can row him acrost Oregon Inlet; then git him back to Skyco by buggy for the steamer sailin'. Where's the girl?"

Mama replied offhandedly, "Gone visitin'."

"Where?"

"Don't know, Filene. We weren't expectin' you this soon."

Filene frowned. "An' you don't know where she is?"

Mama shook her head. "I don't keep too close watch on her now."

Filene turned to me. "Where is she, Ben?"

I stood speechless.

"Speak up, boy," he said.

"Cap'n, I haven't seen her this morning," I said, which was true.

Filene looked at both of us suspiciously, then asked a tricky question. "Why is that dog tied up out there? You never tied him before."

I didn't know what to say but Mama took over.

She laughed. "Next you'll be askin' where Fid is." She stepped over to the window. "Right out there he is. Down by the marsh. Look at him."

Filene didn't budge.

Mama asked, "What's got into you?"

The keeper answered, "What's into me is that I want Ben to go find her an' bring her back to the station, kit packed."

"Ben has to work today," Mama said.

Filene answered, "All right, I'll jus' turn the off-duty crew out an' they'll find her."

"Whatever you say, Cousin," was Mama's answer.

We watched Filene go. He stopped to eye Boo Dog a moment before he went on down the path.

I started to say something but Mama held up her hand. "We best not talk about it," she said. "You might slip an' tell me where she is."

With a case of bad nerves, knowing that Luther Gaskins and Mark Jennette were probably checking door-to-door, north to south, I worked at the Burrus store. Yet I felt Tee was safe for at least another day. Knocking on every door, it would take the surfmen that long to reach Buxton Woods. Even then, if they went to Mis' Creedy's, I had an idea she'd find a way to talk around the subject.

At the same time, I needed information on what was happening at Heron Head Station so I went to Kilbie Oden's house after work and drew him outside. Kilbie could be trusted and was always one to come to the front in emergencies. I told him what I'd done with Teetoncey and why, then said, "I need a spy, Kilbie."

Those light blue eyes lit up.

"I've got to know what Filene is planning and what kind of condition the consul is in. If he's miserable enough he'll leave. If he gets too sick we might have to bury him out here. I'm hoping he'll be just miserable and not deathly; then decide to go back to Norfolk. Soon."

Kilbie nodded. "I'll mosey over to the station after while." Kilbie had been born when the moon was coming to full, which meant he'd be thrifty and probably good at business. He had uncommonly keen intelligence.

I said, "I'll probably ride to Buxton Woods tonight just in case I have to transfer her to that old mill at Big Kinnakeet. If they get close I'll do it. Anyway, see if you can get word to me tomorrow."

Kilbie nodded again, happy to help. But then he eyed me sharply. "You sure you haven't fallen in love with that girl?"

I answered truthfully. "She's been nothing but trouble." I'd been so busy with that girl I hadn't had time to go duck hunting, at which I'm inclined to be good. I also think she was ruining Boo Dog. He didn't even look at ducks anymore. But I still thought Tee could further my purpose, so she was worth the trouble.

When I got home I found that Mama had baked two pumpkin pies. She said, "Whoever is boarding Teetoncey might like these."

I agreed.

After supper I left for Buxton Woods with the pies, spending the night in Mis' Creedy's back room following a long and enjoyable listening to. They discussed London Tower.

After nine in the morning, Kilbie rode up on his papa's mule and just by the bubbling-over looks of his face, I knew he had information. We all chatted a minute and then I went outside with Kilbie.

He said, "That consul *is* sick an' miserable but not dyin'. All he wants to do is git that girl an' leave here. Forever. He's sleepin' in that room with Filene an' is beside himself. You know how hot Filene keeps his room with that kerosene heater, an' how bad he snores . . ."

I nodded.

"Also, the consul is mad at Filene because he can't produce the girl an' now Filene is mad at him. Last night at supper the consul cleaned his specs while the keeper was blessin' the food. An' Filene looked out o' the corners o' his eyes an' caught him. You know that no one moves at that table while Filene is prayin'."

I did know that and had to laugh. The consul couldn't have made a worse mistake. Things were working out fine.

"So Filene wants him to leave, as much as he

wants to go. But . . ." (Kilbie always had an annoying habit of leaving the bad news until last) ". . . there's a problem, Ben. They all figure you're hidin' the girl now, an' Filene thinks he knows how to find her."

"How?"

"He's gonna turn Boo Dog loose this mornin' an' he's bettin' that hound'll come right to Teetoncey."

I steamed. I'd never heard of such a dirty trick. Filene was using my own dog to trap the girl. "I wish that dog would go to Pea Island and stay."

Kilbie said, "If you brought her down here with Fid, an' she didn't walk any of the way, Boo might not be able to track her."

Boo was smarter than that. "He'll get a whiff of Fid and come straight here, and Filene'll be watching every wag of his tail." I could picture the keeper loping along behind Boo as he zigzagged and sniffed his way south.

We sat for a moment on Mis' Creedy's split-rail fence and then Kilbie had an idea. "Why don't I take her to the mill on the mule, an' you walk Fid north in the water for a while, so Boo will lose his scent. Then turn Fid loose. That hound'll circle hisself crazy."

It was a good Kilbie idea, as usual, and we accomplished it, borrowing several blankets from Mis' Creedy plus some food. Teetoncey wasn't upset at leaving Mis' Creedy's, though she had enjoyed staying there. She now looked forward to spending several nights in the mill. I did not tell her that some Hatteras rats also liked to live in that mill, dining on old corn leftovers.

Of course, I was not at Mis' Creedy's when Filene arrived in early afternoon, courtesy of the gold hound. But I heard some of the story later. Mis' Creedy, not wanting to tell a lie, admitted to the keeper that Teetoncey had been there but had gone again, to where she did not know. Then, as Kilbie predicted, Boo went in circles along the edge behind Mis' Creedy's cottage. No one was with Filene so I do not know his reactions but I must guess that he called Boo Dog every possible stupid name, short of cussing him. They deserved each other for trying such an underhanded trick.

There were some tow sacks of cornhusks underneath the millhouse and we carried them up and inside, spreading the husks on the floor for a mattress. Then I found an old bait trap down on the sound bank and brought it up to store our sack of food, so the rats wouldn't change their diet.

Close together under the blankets to keep warm, lying on the floor of the mill on the husks, near the heavy stones that had ground corn for a half century, Tee and I talked a lot that night. There was enough light breeze to make the tattered vanes, tied down so they wouldn't rotate, rattle and creak. We could hear the surf faintly from across the island but being winter, the marsh was quiet. It was very peaceful in the abandoned mill.

"You know, I've never been outside this old Tar Heel state. I want to go everywhere, Tee. I want to see what this world is about. I'm going soon, I swear, and be a cabin boy, then get mate's papers like Reuben and sail for twenty years or so. Then come back here when I'm an old man and be a surfman, like my papa and Filene and Jabez." I'd dreamed of doing this for a long time.

"You really want to leave here?" she asked.

"I cannot wait."

Tee said, "Ben, some people would like to trade lives with you. City dwellers, I mean."

I had to laugh. "Stuck out here on sand, without a railroad; not even a steamship dock within ten miles. Not even a street with a lamp on it. We don't even have a chamber toilet on these islands."

Tee looked over. "There are boys in London who'd give anything to have what you have. I think it's the most exciting place I've ever been."

Maybe she was still daft from hitting her head on the hard bottom in the surf.

"There's nothing out here except birds, fish, sand, and wrecks," I protested.

"It's very beautiful in its own way. You just don't see it."

Just then a rat, about a foot long, came edging down a beam for a look around. His beady eyes glittered.

Tee saw him and sucked a breath. "What's that, Ben?"

Knowing that women do not take very well to rats, I said, "Just an old beautiful coon snooping around."

Her voice was jumpy. "What's a coon?"

"Raccoon. I used to have one. Tame."

I slammed the palm of my hand into the floor boards, raising some dust that made us both sneeze, and the fellow took off. He'd be back, I knew, but I had not heard of these Hatteras rats biting any live human so they weren't anything to worry about.

We talked on and then went to sleep.

While there are vicious storms in the winter, there are also gentle rains that fall on the Banks. The skies lower down without a cloud boil anywhere; the rains fall for a day or two, filling the cisterns and giving the sparse vegetation a welcome drink without drowning it.

I woke up just after dawn to a *pitter-pat* and a *drip-drop*, getting splashed on the cheek. The roof was leaking from a dozen places and I looked out through the cracks at early gray light.

It was going to be a damp, cold, miserable day, I knew. Some cornhusks could plug the holes in the roof but trying to heat the place was something else.

Tee was still asleep and I eased out from under the blankets, pulled on my shoes and went outside, down the short ladder. After answering nature's call, shivering a little, I stuffed my jacket pockets with husks and climbed up to the edge of the roof. There was no way to find those holes in the wet shingles and I gave up on that. But there was an old lard tin under the housing for a make-do stove and some scraps of wood. Then it dawned on me that I had no matches nor a way to start a fire. I kicked the tin away and climbed back into the millhouse.

Tee had awakened and was sitting up. She said, "It's leaking in here, Ben."

"Is that so?" I said, feeling none too good.

Mama was now putting on breakfast in the dry warmth of our kitchen. Filene was eating grits and sausage gravy in the dry warmth of the station, and we were stuck out in a wet mill.

Tee went out to answer her own call and I sat

down on the edge of the framework around the grinding wheel, promptly getting hit in the top of the head with a cold drop. When she got back, looking a little soggy, I said, "Pass me up some husks," and climbed into the rafters, which were loaded with mud nests for waspies, to plug the leaks. That took about twenty minutes. We weren't speaking very much. While I was up there, she asked, "Will this rain last long?"

I answered, "Ask the rain."

After I was down, she said, as a complaining woman, "I'm cold, Ben."

I said, "Well, heat a brick and stick it in your frock." I was just as cold.

She stared at me and that made me even madder. I said, "We got no tweeny maids out here. You have to take care of yourself."

She didn't say anything but huddled like an orphan in a blanket while I got out what food was left. Cold livermush sandwiches. On biting into hers, she made a face and I blew up.

"You should have brought your cook from London."

It went on that way for a while and then a rat scampered across the floor. She shrieked and I got really disgusted. "Stop yelling," I said. "Nothing but a rat."

Teetoncey let loose, little white lines of anger around her eyes. Try as I might, as good Methodists should do, I cannot easily forget what she called me: A "naughty, mean, rude, selfish, thoughtless oaf." That was not all. She also screamed, "I wouldn't stay another moment in that smelly house, in your smelly room, and your smelly bed, eating this awful food, if it weren't for the silver . . ."

Then she clapped her hand over her mouth as if the Hatteras cat had just jumped out.

What silver? I thought. *Now, what was that about?*

I couldn't inquire. Teetoncey was now toppled over in sobs that must have been wrenching her ribs. I stood there a moment, plagued by the thing that plagues all men—a crying woman. I am not always mean and selfish and I mustered up and went to her, touching the blanket and saying I was sorry about the rat. I sat down by her. It was miserable and damp enough in that mill without a lot of hysterical tears.

I said, "I know it's cold in here and I wish we had eggs for breakfast..." I didn't know what else to say to her. However, I suppose that was plenty, a gesture of some friendship on my part. She raised her head and sniffed and swallowed; sniffed a little more, wiped her eyes and nose, and pretty soon said, "Ben, I didn't mean to call you those names. I do sincerely apologize." So British.

I accepted.

After a short time, sitting close to her, a blanket around me now, I got back to what was still on my mind. "You said something about silver..."

Tee was silent a moment and then sighed deeply before unburdening her heavy secret. "You remember I said my father chartered the *Malta Empress* to take us to Barbados and back to New York?"

I nodded.

"We went there so my father could sell his holdings. They were inherited but he could not manage them from London. They included sugar plantation land, a molasses factory, and a rum distillery. Our estate was in Christ Church, between Ealing Grove and Graeme Hall, a very lovely place. It's in the tropics, Ben, so warm and green. I would have preferred to live there but we couldn't. Anyway, the estate shipped dark crystal sugar, white crystals, pan molasses, rum . . ."

Sitting in the drafty mill, listening to her, I decided I'd have to visit the Barbadoes someday.

"We stayed four months and then a Dutchman sailed over from Curaçao and bought the estate for twenty thousand pounds."

Pounds of what? "What's a pound?" I asked.

"A sovereign. Twenty shillings. Each pound is equal to about five American dollars."

I figured quickly. That was a lot of money. About a hundred thousand dollars. You could buy the whole state of North Carolina for that much. Maybe South Carolina, too.

"The Dutchman paid us in East India silver bar, *bullion,* and my father placed it in two chests . . . and about a week later we boarded the *Empress* near the careenage in Bridgetown . . ."

"What's a careenage?"

"Part of the port where they tilt ships to work on them."

Tee knew more about the sea than I thought. "Go on," I said.

"Then we sailed. A few days later, my father, in a jolly mood and laughing, said, 'Wendy, in case a carriage runs us down in New York, keep an eye on those chests. There's a fortune in them, as you know.'"

I had to ask, "Were they aboard when you hit Heron Shoal?" She nodded. We'd had a Boston vessel, the *Richard Kent*, founder with twenty thousand in gold on it. Now, a hundred thousand in silver. "You sure, Teetoncey?"

She nodded again.

If the cracks in the mill floor had been wide enough, I would have plummeted to sand. A hundred thousand dollars was sitting on a bar not more than three miles from our house.

7

I WAS NO LONGER cold or damp or miserable, seeing the possibility of a fortune before I reached the age of thirteen. But there were some problems and they were large ones. I said, "Tee, of all the places in the world to drop a hundred thousand in silver, this might have been the worst."

"Why?" she asked.

I shook my head. "Long before us Outer Bankers were lifesavers, we were wreckers. Salvage people. It still runs deep in the blood. After a ship wrecks, I've seen people root around like wild hogs for ten dollars in gold coins. These Banks are poor. If it was known that much silver was on Heron, they'd shovel a hole to China to get it."

"What shall I do?" Teetoncey asked.

I didn't rightfully know at the moment but just then I heard a loon cry. I knew Kilbie was out there somewhere because it had always been our signal in times when we needed to communicate that way. I walked over, creaked the door open, and gave him a laughing gull screech. In a moment, he came up on his papa's mule. He was sensibly dressed in a sou'wester and rubber coat but that brown mule was pretty wet. I beckoned Kilbie in.

He climbed up and said "Howdy" to Teetoncey and then said to me, "I think your troubles are over, Ben. The consul left this mornin', telling the keeper that Wendy Appleton could stay here the rest of her life so far as he was concerned. He was mighty upset, Ben. Mad at everybody. He had to get back to Norfolk after wasting three days and getting an awful cold."

"He left in this rain?"

Kilbie nodded. "Filene borrowed the Farrow buggy, fitted him out with oilskins, an' got him on his way overland. They'll row him across Oregon Inlet. I think it's lucky he got off the Banks alive. He called Filene an ignorant peasant last night . . ."

Consul Calderham *was* lucky. So far as I knew, Filene would jerk an oak tree out for less than that. I felt a great weight off all of us. I said, "That's good news, Kilbie."

Kilbie added, "Filene is still roastin' about you but he'll calm down in a day or two, Jabez said."

I looked over at Teetoncey. She was smiling and happy again. "Can we go home now?" she asked. Home, was it? Maybe it wasn't so smelly after all?

"I guess," I said. Throughout this conversation, the silver had been in the back of my mind. It would be impossible for Tee and myself to salvage it alone. We'd need help.

"Can I tell Kilbie?" I asked Tee. She knew what I was talking about.

"If you think it's wise," she answered.

"Sit down, Kilbie," I said, and he arranged himself on the framework of the grinding wheel. I then told him about the East India bullion on Heron Shoal and how it got there. He reacted as I expected, with a whistle and a "Jumpin' Jehoshaphat."

I asked, "What do you know about salvage rights?"

"Not much," Kilbie replied. "But if we git it up out o' there, it should be ours."

I had not had time to discuss shares with Teetoncey but assumed she would do the right thing if we helped her save the chests. In my mind, already, it would not have to be equal. If she'd give us, say, twenty-five thousand dollars for our efforts, then she'd be welcome to the rest, particularly since she was without living kin in England. I also had in mind bringing Frank Scarborough along. She would still have seventy-five thousand dollars, which is more than enough to last a lifetime for a girl of twelve. The rest of us would share a "fee," coming out at an eight thousand odd lot each.

I pointed out to Kilbie that we'd have to plan it carefully. "Wait for the lowest tide of the month, until we can see that sandbar clean of water, then hope it's a calm day."

Teetoncey said, "Those chests are very heavy, Ben."

I waved that aside. "Once we get to them, we'll hitch a line to Fid and let him pull them out."

Kilbie said, "It's worth a try."

Then I looked at both of them sternly. "Besides Frank, we can't tell a soul. There'd be a ruckus out here beyond belief."

Kilbie agreed.

We all three got on the dripping brown mule and rode toward my house in the rain.

Boo Dog was barking his head off from inside when we pulled up, and then swarmed all over Teetoncey when I opened the door. He favored me a slight greeting.

Mama was also very pleased to see us, especially Teetoncey, and ran to fix us some dinner. She made Tee get out of her wet clothes immediately and started to heat water for a kitchen bath in the tin tub. She apparently thought I had not undergone the same miserable rigors in the cold and damp of that millhousing. I had to fend for myself.

Later, she got me aside and said, "I do deceive we shouldn't have done what we did. It was almost kidnappin', an' it's been on my mind for three days now. After being proud to live as the Bible tells me, I have to confess to Filene it was all my ideer."

Truthfully speaking, it was *her* idea and maybe that would get me off the hook with Keeper Midgett.

However, I had more to do than worry about hot tub baths and Cousin Filene. As soon as I dried off and changed clothes, I went to the almanac to check low tides for January and February 1899. We'd need one when the Atlantic, at full moon, sucked every available inch of water off Heron Head Shoal.

At supper that night, after we bowed for grace and before we started eating, Teetoncey said, "You've both been so good to me that I have something to say. I've been so worried about it. I feel so guilty." I thought—Tee, if you tell her about the silver I'll punch you right in the mouth.

Not looking at us, and showing her guilt, I suppose, Tee said, "I told a lie that first night, but I didn't really mean to. I said I had no relatives in England. I do."

We both stared at her.

"I have an uncle," she confessed. "Mother's brother, who lives with his family in Chelsea. His name is Salisbury. He's a hateful man and I dislike him very much, and I don't like his children. I do not want to live with him . . ." Then she looked direct at Mama. "I think that's why I said I had no family."

I felt the fool. Here, I'd told everybody she was a complete orphan, gaining a lot of sympathy. Now, she wasn't.

Mama was shocked, too, but when the shock wore off, she said, "We understand, Tee."

My head spun for the second time that day. There was a lot more to Teetoncey than met the eye. In bed, after four or five tortured sighs, Mama said, "I guess we'll have to tell Filene."

I said, "Mama, let's don't rush into it." I'd had

some time to think. Tee's uncle would scurry aboard the *Lucania* if he knew a hundred thousand in bullion was sitting on our shore. Fare thee well for shares.

In the morning, though I knew it was against her principles, Mama finally agreed that what Tee's uncle Salisbury didn't temporarily know would not hurt him. There was also the likelihood that he had no knowledge that the Appletons were aboard the *Malta Empress*, although Lloyds of London had probably posted the wreck by now. And what Filene Midgett didn't know certainly would not hurt him, either.

8

NEXT DAY, the sun came brightly back over the Banks and just before low tide, I met Kilbie and Frank Scarborough on the beach at Heron Head Shoal. We stood and looked out toward the sandbar, which was about eight hundred yards offshore. With the tide ebbing, it was still covered.

"Where do you think she hit?" Kilbie asked.

"Teetoncey or the *Malta Empress*?" I asked.

"The bark," Kilbie said. "If you know just about where she smacked on that shoal, then we can go right to the spot."

I didn't know.

"Well, where did you find the girl?"

I walked a ways and then looked around. "Right about here."

Kilbie took a piece of driftwood and stuck it up in the bank just about opposite where I was standing. The current had been setting south that night so it meant that the *Empress* had been three or four hundred yards up from this spot.

I paced off three hundred fifty giant steps and then said, "She should have hit about straight out from here." It was only a guess.

Frank marked that spot with another piece of driftwood and we sat down to wait for the tide to expose the shoal. There wasn't much surf that day and we'd soon be able to take a good look at the bar, for what it was worth.

Scanning out, I said, "It's a shame that not one measly piece of that keel nor a length of ribbing got stuck out there. Then we'd know exactly where to look."

Kilbie had been quiet and thoughtful for a few minutes. Finally he said, "It might be impossible. Those chests could have worked themselves ten feet down into sand."

While Kilbie was running all sorts of negative problems through his mind, Frank and I just had blind faith we'd find the chests. Faith of any kind is what counts.

About twenty minutes later, the water fell to maybe an inch on the shoal, which was about a quarter mile long and varied in width from thirty to forty feet, a mound of sand that dropped off sharp on the east edge, leaving westerly water about two fathoms deep all the way to the surf line, then shallowing out at a fathom and sloping, finally, to the beach.

From where we sat there was nothing to be seen on top of that shoal—not that I hadn't already looked at it numerous times in previous passings. But there was always the possibility that a nub of something would be washed clean of sand overnight, bob up like a surfacing whale. After a storm, pieces of ancient wrecks sometimes come to light as if they'd made a voyage through sand to the bottom of the earth and returned.

I said, "We'll just take my boat, go out there, and probe around." But I now believed it was silly to think Fid could pull those chests out with a line from shore. I'd thought about taking him out in the small boat with us but felt that might end up in a mess.

Kilbie disencouraged any miracles. He said solemnly, "Only chance we got is to figure everthin' an' map it all out. Ben, you pick a date but watch out for the tide. Frank—we'll need some line and buoys." It never failed. Kilbie somehow always got himself into command.

By now, the bar was out of water enough to accommodate a flight of pecking, prancing gulls, and we couldn't even see a shattered rail stub out there.

Frank and I went on to Chicky village. I had to work and Frank was going to hang around the store until his papa docked about four o'clock with a catch.

Just before supper, I told Teetoncey what we'd done during the day; that Kilbie was going to start paperwork, which he dearly loved. She wanted to know if she could help.

Later, I said.

I wasn't at all sure what she could do. Salvage work, of which there is no meaner, is not for women.

Weather conditions willing, it seemed to me that January 16 would be the ideal date to do a little secret probing on Heron Head Shoal. The almanac calculated we'd have a full moon that night, with a high tide at 8:06 P.M. Go back six hours and we should be in position on that bar at 1 P.M. and wait for the tide to go to its lowest some sixty minutes later.

I wondered how low the water would be at that time of year, and not knowing very much about tides, except that they went up and down, I took a trip to the Lifesaving Station on the following day to contact Mark Jennette. While Jabez had more beach experience than Mark, he was not very scholarly. Jennette had passed his exams as a mate and had sailed awhile on a couple of schooners.

I found him on duty in the lookout cupola, with UDT, his big gray cat. That was a strange name for a cat, just three initials, and Mark said it meant *Underwater Delirium Tremens,* or the "three fathom shakes." But everyone thought it had a deeper meaning.

"What do you know about tides?" I asked.

Mark, stroking his brownish-red mustache, replied, "Well, they rise and fall."

I knew that. "How long do they stay slack, when they're not rising and falling?"

"That depends," Mark said.

That's a rotten word. "On what?"

"Moon, sun, atmospheric pressure; onshore wind, offshore wind . . ." Mark saw me frowning and said, "Keep watch for me." There was a steamer going north; a barentine headed south. Sea, calm; wind in its usual prevail, west of south. There wasn't much to "lookout" from that tower.

Mark went down the ladder and soon came back with a thick tan book. "This is the greatest book ever written," he said. (Mama would argue the point and stick with the Holy Bible.) "It's by Nathaniel Bowditch."

He read, "The cause of the tides is the periodic disturbance of the ocean from its position of equilibrium brought about through the periodic differences of attraction upon water particles of the earth by the moon, and to a lesser degree by the sun . . ."

More or less, I knew that. He read on and finally got to the part which confirmed my January 16 date. ". . . at times of new and full moon, the highest high tides and the lowest low tides are experienced . . ."

That was it. "Is January better than February or March?" I asked.

He read again. "Tides will be increased by the sun's action when the earth is near its perihelion, about January 1 . . ."

"Peri what?" I asked.

"Perihelion. I'm not sure what it is but it appears that tides are lower and higher in January than in July."

That was perfect. Tee would be long gone by July.

I asked again: "How long do they stay slack?" A very important question so far as Heron bar was concerned.

Mark laughed. "That depends. Jabez says they

stay slack long enough for a gull to digest a perch an' clean his wings. That's about right."

Stroking his cat, Mark asked, "Ben, why do you want to know all this information?" The cat's big yellowish eyes were boring in on me.

I said, "So I can discuss it with Teetoncey."

I thanked Mark and wound down through the messroom. Filene was sitting at the crew's table, specs on nose, reading a copy of the Norfolk *Virginian-Pilot*. He glanced up and gave me a look that was enough to close my windpipe but didn't say anything. I went on my way to Kilbie's house to report what I'd learned.

The year came to a close.

New Christmas, December 25, which all the mainlanders seemed to celebrate, was filtering very slowly to the Outer Banks but we paid more attention to the eve of January 6, Old Christmas, which was the traditional celebration for as long as anyone knew. Let the mainlanders play with sacred dates. Busybodies, they were ruining our post office names but had to let Christmas alone. It was now the Year of Our Lord, 1899.

On Christmas Eve afternoon, Mama, Tee, Fid, Boo Dog, and myself went to Chicky village to watch Kilbie and his brother, Everett, run around in cow heads and hide draped to their waist. They were pretending to be Old Buck, the wild bull of Trent Woods. The program did not vary from year to year. Tee seemed to be baffled by the whole thing, which surprised me, since we had inherited our Christmas from England. Then we went home and had a festive evening.

Every few days, while waiting for the calendar to tick off January 16, we were meeting in the hulk of the *Hettie Carmichael,* sheltered from the wind, to discuss the silver salvage. Of course, we were also sheltered from snooping eyes.

On this particular day, Kilbie had brought a sketch along. It showed the sandbar and had a pair of straight lines penciled across to mark the area where we thought the *Empress* had piled up.

Kilbie showed it to Tee and asked, "Where did your papa keep the chests?"

"In the cabin with us. They're extraordinarily

heavy, Kilbie. It took four men with ropes and planks to get them down the ladder."

Kilbie nodded and drew the outline of a vessel in the sand. "Now show me where the cabin was."

Tee stuck her finger down. It appeared to be a bit forward of midships. Kilbie studied it a moment and then drew an X on his sketch. "That's where the chests are," he said confidently.

I said, "Kilbie, how do you know that the *Empress* didn't slew around after she hit?" I'd seen a half dozen ships that rammed a sandbar head-on and then went sideways when the seas caught them. They never stayed head on.

"All right," he said. "If we don't find them here we take the X and move it forty feet in this direction or forty feet in that direction."

It was very hard to beat Kilbie.

We then began to gather equipment. Frank stole some line from his papa and made three buoys out of gallon glass jugs that had good stoppers in them. He also took an old boat hook and hacksawed the prong off, leaving the metal tip so we'd have something to probe with. There is a different feel when you hit soggy wood underwater than when you hit metal. Frank then found a long, thin pole and remounted the altered boat hook.

I worked on the *Me and the John O'Neal.* I unstepped the mast and made sure all the oakum caulking in the seams was secure; checked the oar pins and rounded up all the spare line I could find; checked my anchor. Kilbie's plan was to buoy the chests and then come back on the next low tide, raise them up and then float them ashore under some barrels. Kilbie seemed to have learned something about salvage already.

Teetoncey asked what she could do. "You're in charge of the food," I said. I couldn't think of any other assignment for her. We'd have to be on the beach by midmorning, eat something, and then be ready to row out to Heron Head about one o'clock.

Meanwhile, as time hastened on, I kept checking the barometer. The weather was pretty stable that second week of January, just as the almanac had predicted. I bet I read that almanac fifty times between Old Christmas and January 15, a Sunday.

January, 1899—1st to 3rd. Storm period generally. Storms out of southwest move across southland. 4th to 7th—Cold spell. Storms clear in North Atlantic states. Light snow in Rockies to Kansas-Nebraska. Showers on Pacific coast. Some snow on south plateau to west Texas. 8th to 11th—Unsettled time. Showers along the Gulf coast up through Maryland. Mostly fair in California. 11th to 15th—Stormy from Pacific states to Great Lakes but generally fair and mild in mid-Atlantic states. 16th to 19th—Heavy snow New England states but mild in mid-Atlantic states . . .

Mid-Atlantic was us. I did not know how the rest of the country was faring but it was sure fine along the Hatteras Banks, almost like May weather. Whoever does the forecasting for the almanac is an expert.

I think it is true that a maternal instinct exists because Mama asked me several times, when she caught me studying the almanac or checking the barometer, if something was going on. On the 15th, she said, "Ben, I do deceive that you an' Tee are goin' behind my back. I feel it an' I smell it." There was no way to smell what we were doing, even with her big nose, but feeling was possible.

I went so far as saying, "Mama, we're working on something that's going to give you a life of ease. By Groundhog Day, you'll have a crank washing machine right in this kitchen."

Mama said frankly, "I'd a sight rather have you in high school in Manteo," and then went on about her business, but worriedly, I think.

That same nice night Tee and I went out on the porch and looked at the moon just after it rose. While I knew a lot about the moon I did not know enough to judge when it was absolutely chock o' block full. But it looked like that last sliver was already in place. If so, that would mean another million gallons of water would drain off Heron Head Shoal on the morrow.

Tee laughed when I addressed the moon: "Suck every drop off that sandbar."

She was impressed with my knowledge of the moon, courtesy Reuben, that it took seven days to go from first quarter to full; two weeks to shrink from full to new; that *perigee* was when it was closest to the earth and *apogee* made it far out. But there is much about the moon that none of us know.

There were seven hundred bushels of stars out that night and aside from admiring them I found out she'd never thought much about them. It was dim but I showed her Job's Coffin; then Aldebaran and old Betelgeuse, or as Reuben says, "Ol' Beetlejuice."

Then we went to bed but neither of us really slept soundly.

9

IN THE MORNING, Kilbie and Frank came down to the house but kept out of sight, meeting Tee and me down at the dock. Checking back to see if Mama was prying around near the windows, we quickly loaded the boat on the pony cart, then got the buoys, probe, and line that they'd stashed away nearby. Tee had stealthily made some food the previous night and we stuck that on the seat, then got under way for Heron Head, Boo Dog padding along behind to continue his wooing of the castaway girl.

Arriving at the beach, we were relieved to find that there wasn't a soul around. With the fine weather, no lifesaving patrols were out and it wasn't likely any would come along. Most of the traffic this time of year went inside on the trails along the sound. With luck, we could go about our work undisturbed.

We unloaded the boat and carried it down to the beach opposite where Frank had driven the piece of driftwood into the sand. Then Kilbie scanned his sketch. It appeared we were in the correct position to reach his first X mark but the bar was still covered with water. Tide was ebbing fast but it would be another two hours before we launched.

I was glad to see that there wasn't much surf. Maybe two feet rolling in gently from the Atlantic. It couldn't have been a better day, cloudless except for a few fluffs on the far horizon.

With everything ready, we went up to sit on the bank and wait. We talked awhile about the sandbar and raising the chests but even that got boring. Then Frank, who had a mean streak in him at times, asked Teetoncey, "You ever heerd boys cuss?"

She frowned a little. "I've heard our gardener's boy curse several times."

Frank nodded to Kilbie to start it off. Kilbie said, "Tarnation."

I said, "Hell."

Frank said, "Hellfire."

Kilbie said, "Damn."

I said, "Double damn."

Frank said, "Damnation."

We looked at Teetoncey and she seemed to be disgusted, which is exactly what we'd hoped to achieve. She got up and walked a few paces, then turned swiftly and yelled, "Bloody bawstard."

We three almost fell off the bank. We thought we knew what that last word meant but we'd never used it. Then she laughed as if she had chimes in her throat, which made it worse. That girl had a fouler mouth than I'd ever expected and should stay away from the gardener's boy. We didn't have much to do with her until it came time to eat.

Boo Dog went over and sat down beside her since he was never easily offended.

About one o'clock, when we could start to see the outline of the bar under the white froth on top, we got ready to launch. Thinking about what had happened at this very spot in early November, I asked Tee, "You sure you want to come out with us?"

"Yes," she said, though she was beginning to be a little nervous.

I got into the boat, sat down on the center thwart, and dropped the oars between the gunwale tholes. Water lapped at the bow. Then Tee got in; crawled around me to go to the bow. I said to Frank and Kilbie, "Shove on out."

They pushed and we slid into the water and I heaved on the oars, riding up on the first swell. We went nicely, taking the second one without getting much water aboard. Heaving hard, I shot us on past the surf line and we were in deep water, headed for the shoal. I angled north to go around the far end of the bar, then drift down to about opposite our driftwood stake onshore.

Frank said, "See how easy it is."

Always cautious, Kilbie replied, "Don't speak too soon."

I was busy on the oars and Tee remained silent; fearful, I'm sure, of stepping foot on that patch of sand that had doomed the *Empress* and her folks.

In another few minutes, we were about on a line with the driftwood stake and Kilbie said, "Keep her steady, Ben," and then instructed Tee to heave the anchor up on the bar. I thought Frank should do it but Tee tossed it up, hooking the bar like an old salt.

"Pay some line out," I yelled at her.

I glanced back. She was behaving like a sailor.

Soon, *Me and the John O'Neal* rode about forty feet off the shoal, pulled seaward by the ebbing tide.

We began looking closely as the water, with each lap, left a little more of the sand mound exposed to the blue sky. The weather was holding and there wasn't more than three knots of listless breeze.

Tee then startled us by remembering something. "The chests were tied with thick rope to each other, and then to the mast where it went through the cabin."

Kilbie said, "That makes sense. So they wouldn't shift around when the bark rolled or pitched."

That did make sense.

"But I don't see any stubs of masts anywhere," Frank said, straining his eyes to look over the surface of the bar, which had no more than three inches of water on it now.

Kilbie said, "I'm sorry to bust your bubbles but I think those chests are twenty feet down in sand."

I refused to be defeated. I said, "Let's heave in and get up on that bar." They heaved up on the line and in a moment the prow touched the bar.

Looking toward shore, Tee said anxiously, "I hope the boat doesn't get away from us."

I glanced across the eight hundred yards of smooth, low rolling, green-blue ocean and answered, "If it does we got a long, cold swim." I then double-checked the anchor line to make certain it was secure to the bow ring. After that, we all got out with Frank carrying the probe; I carried the glass jug buoys. Then we began to slosh over the bar, which was now covered with no more than an inch of water.

Kilbie looked down and around; then shook his head. "I'm standin' on the X and I don't see a thing."

Neither did I. There were some white chips of shells in the water-pooled small sand valleys, ridges and ripples on the bar. Otherwise, it was as clean as our kitchen floor.

Frank drove the probe down an inch from Kilbie's toes and it went in about a foot; then he had to work it back and forth to sink it deeper. Finally, it went down to about three feet. He pulled it out and stuck it in again closer to where I was standing. In five minutes, Frank had probed two more holes without touching so much as a broken conch.

"I don't think it's here," he said.

Kilbie pulled his sketch out and paced forty feet north. "Try here."

We moved up there and Frank rammed the long pole with the metal tip back into the sand, working it and pushing it down. By now, the bar was out of water.

"How much longer we got?" Kilbie asked.

I looked over the side of the bar. The tide was still dropping but wouldn't go down more than another inch or two. "Not much longer than it'll take a gull to digest a perch and clean his wings," quoting Jabez accurately, via Mark Jennette.

Kilbie gave me a pained look.

While all this was going on, Luther Gaskins was up in the Heron Head lookout with his long glass. Much to his surprise, he picked up some foolish people standing on the shoal. A small boat was seen to be anchored to the bar. A light-coated dog was seen to be running around the beach, positively identifying us. (That dog was becoming a Jonah.) With the sea calm and the breeze light, Luther decided not to tell the keeper, knowing of my recent troubles.

Meanwhile, we'd made at least ten probes into the X spot marked to the north on Kilbie's sketch.

Nothing! Not a scrap of keel, rib, or deck planking; not a boom, block, or bumpkin. The *Malta Empress*, if there was anything left of her at all, was not in this spot.

About twenty minutes had now passed and I looked over the edge of the bar. Slack water was done and the tide was creeping back up again. I said uneasily, "We got ten minutes at best."

"Let's move south," said Kilbie and we ran that way, Kilbie pacing off forty feet from the spot where we'd first probed.

Frank stuck the depronged boat hook in again and still another time. On his third try, he shouted, "Hot damn! I hit metal." He rapped it down several times. Then I tried it. Kilbie, too. It was metal, all right.

Kilbie and I dropped down to our knees and began to claw sand near the probe hole. Frank joined us. Out of the corner of my eye, I saw Tee just standing there and looking like a ghost was at her throat. I yelled, "Dig," and she got down with us but wasn't happy about it.

Anybody who has ever dug in wet sand on a

shoal or along the beach knows that water and sand slime come in about as fast as you can get the hard sand out, but we managed to go down about two feet. Then my hand touched something.

"Dig," I yelled. We had it! With my blind faith, I was sure we were close to silver.

But in a few seconds, we exposed what seemed to be an iron ring about a foot in diameter. It was stuffed with sand and seemed to go straight down. We scraped away another two or three inches and Kilbie, disheartened, said, "This is just an iron pipe, probably off another ship."

I got mad. "Dig, anyway."

Just about that time, I felt water lapping at my toes. Over my shoulder, I could see that the tide was beginning to creep back across Heron Head Shoal. As I began to claw more sand I felt something on the top of my skull. It was burrowing into the marrow. I looked over toward the beach and, unmistakably, Mama stood on the shore. Her falcon eyes had carried eight hundred yards.

That woman had not been to the beach for ten years, ever since my papa capsized. She hated the ocean passionately. Going to Heron Head Station, she'd always look up island or down island or inland; never out at the sea. But now she was on the beach and I could think of nothing more forbidding.

I sat back on my haunches, sighed, and said, "Wouldn't you know it?"

"Who is it?" Kilbie asked. He had short vision.

"Mama."

He groaned. "I thought she took naps on winter afternoons."

"Not since Teetoncey got here."

Tee said sharply, "It's not my fault."

Ignoring her, I said, "Quick, let's put a buoy on that pipe."

Frank ran to get one and I located a rivet hole and jerked the line through, then tied it off with about thirty feet of slack. We could spot that glass jug easy next time.

I glanced back toward the beach. Mama was just waiting. Not yelling. That made it worse.

"Let's go," I said, trying to think of some worthy explanation to make when we reached shore

Frank pulled the boat up to the bar and jerked

the anchor loose while I manned the oars. Tee and Kilbie got in; then Frank shoved off and jumped in. By now, the bar was awash again.

As I began to row south, Kilbie asked the inevitable question. "What are we gonna tell her, Ben?"

"Tell her we just went out to see the shoal."

"Do you think she'll believe that?"

"Probably not," I answered, but I couldn't figure out anything else. Whatever I said, Mama would raise a ruckus—us taking Teetoncey out on the open ocean. For the moment, we'd forgotten all about the iron pipe.

Then Kilbie brought it up. "What do you think that was, Ben?"

"Just a piece of pipe," I said, thoroughly upset at finding nothing and having the tide catch us; having Mama waiting in dubious welcome.

Tee spoke up. "Could it have been off the boiler for the donkey steam engine?"

I almost dropped the oars, swiveling my head around to look at her. I'd forgotten all about that steam engine that was used to run the pumps on the *Empress;* the boiler that was flooded when a heavy sea boarded.

Kilbie asked, "What donkey engine?"

"It was used for the pumps and the boiler had a stack on it, I remember," Tee said, displaying far more knowledge than I ever expected from one who didn't go to sea.

Kilbie and Frank were perched directly in front of me on the stern seat. I said in a hushed voice, "Boys, we were standing on the *Malta Empress.* That was the broke-off boiler stack."

Kilbie was almost reverent. "I do think we were on top her."

"Not a word to anybody," I ordered and glanced around at Tee. She nodded.

Kilbie then spoke to her. "If you can show me where the boiler was located, then we can git right to the silver. I'll work out the distances."

"Tomorrow," I said, having lost thoughts of the Widow O'Neal standing on the shore with her arms folded.

A few minutes later, I pointed the bow of the *Me and the John O'Neal* direct west and heaved away on the oars. "What's Mama doing?" I asked. My back was to the beach, of course.

Frank answered. "She's walking down to about where we'll land." The current was setting south.

Oh, my. There was only one thing to do—get our ears burned and lug the boat back across the strip. But at least I wanted to show Mama I knew how to handle a boat. I wasn't John O'Neal's son for nothing.

We were almost to the surf line and I saw the first swell grow on the stern. They'd gotten a little bigger since we'd shoved off for the sandbar.

"How am I doing?" I asked Kilbie.

"Just keep her bow headed in."

We lifted and skidded down as the first swell passed under us; then I saw the second one boiling in on us. To this day, I do not know how I got catawampus on that second swell but suddenly we were quartering; then I was sideways in a third one, and we dumped about ten feet from shore.

As I got a face full of cold sea, I saw legs and arms flying, then went under and tumbled away from the boat, gasping at the icy water. When I came up, I saw Mama floundering around in the surf to get Teetoncey. Kilbie was already staggering out and Frank was on his hands and knees, crawling out.

Meanwhile, Boo Dog was running around barking at everyone as if this was a big joke. I yelled at him to shut up and went back into the water to get my boat.

10

I was dry-docked for two weeks.

(1) I was not to go near enough that boat to spit on it. (2) I was not to go near the Atlantic Ocean. (3) I was to do my chores at the Burrus store and come straight home. (4) I was not so much as to get Teetoncey's socks damp or the Widow O'Neal would have Filene strop me. He had not stropped me since the age of nine but I well remembered that cow leather hitting my bare mooney.

Despite all this, the four of us made a solemn

pact not to tell anyone about the bullion and try again on the next full moon, maybe at night so that no one would snoop around. However, the whole experience had left me with grave doubts about the salvaging of that silver. It was deep in the sand, probably lost forever to mankind in general.

During these two weeks of being up on chocks, restricted so to speak, I almost got to know Teetoncey. I discovered she had some definite things in mind about her future. Tee and I didn't really do too much during the fortnight except talk. How could we, jailed in the yard area with the Widow O'Neal plying her chores not more than fifty feet away?

I took it for granted that Tee would have to go within a few months, no matter the British consul's distaste for ever coming back to Heron Head. He could make arrangements via the Lifesaving Service. I also took it for granted that Uncle Salisbury, who did sound hateful and greedy, from all that Tee had said, would be trying to get his hands on the Appleton estate.

"My father has some barrister friends and I shall go to them for advice," she said.

"You going to live in that big four-storied house all by yourself?" I asked.

"I'd like to. I'm very good friends with our household servants. I think I could manage very well."

"Those servants stay right in the house?"

She nodded. "Oh, yes. In the basement and attic."

Well, I guess it was possible that a twelve-year-old girl could do that—run an estate. At any rate, Tee did not seem to have fear of it.

"I could go to school and then come home in the afternoon and see to everything. I might need help with the finances."

"Well, you're sure not poor."

"I don't mean that, Ben. Maybe Barclays would make the schedules." She said "shed-yules."

"Barclays?"

"That's our bank."

There was a bank up in Manteo but most

people on the sand strips wouldn't let them man-age a penny. "Watch out you don't get robbed," I warned.

She smiled. "I shall."

I got to thinking about her running her own life, not having to answer to anyone; doing what she wanted to do and when. It was just possible that she'd come on luck when her parents went loo'ard.

"What'll you do when you're not managing the house?" I asked.

"Oh, go to the theatre. To the Haymarket or Lyceum, or to Royal Albert Hall for the opera. Mums took me now and then."

"Out in the carriage?"

She nodded.

"Or I could go ice-skating in St. James' Park. You should have seen it four years ago. It was frozen for a month."

"You ride those buses with seats on the roof?" After seeing nothing but pony carts and mule wagons, the buses had caught my fancy.

She laughed. "They're very funny. We call

them knifeboard buses. Everyone sits back-to-back on the roof. They've got advertisements all over the rear. Pears Soap, Horlick's Malted Milk, Remington Typewriters, Heinz 57 Soup . . ."

"You got Heinz over there?"

"Yes."

It was a small world. We sold Heinz cans down at the Burrus store.

"And what'll you do at night?" I asked.

"I'll read poetry by Elizabeth Barrett Browning or embroider, same as Mums." A slight look of sadness passed her face, and I knew she was remembering.

"And you'll live there the rest of your life?"

"Oh, I don't think so. I shan't be an old maid, Ben. I shall marry and have children. I want two boys and two girls, so they won't be an only child like I've been. I so much wanted a sister or brother . . ."

Looking at her that day, I just could not connect Teetoncey and a midwife, but I suppose that, too, was possible in the future. She could gain some weight and do it all right.

Then she asked me, "Do you plan to get married?"

"Yeh, when I'm about forty. I don't need any baggage until then."

"That's awfully late," she said.

Late or never. Jabez was forty and hadn't married and seemed perfectly happy. He darned his own socks as well as any woman could do it; sewed his britches' splits, and no one at Heron Head Station complained of his cooking when it was his turn.

"It must be nice to have a brother," she said, changing the subject away from marriage since it was a dead end with me.

"I don't see Reuben very much, but I like him. I just wish he'd talk more when he got home."

"You don't love him?" she asked.

I had to laugh. "How do you love a man?"

"If it's your father or your brother you love him just as well as you love your mother or sister."

I had to think a moment. "I believe I would have loved my papa if I'd known him. From everything I've heard, he was the finest man that ever walked these beaches."

She was silent for a while, then asked, "Why don't you ever hug or kiss your mother? Or say something nice to her?"

I almost fell off the porch. I flustered up. "Boys my age just don't go around hugging and kissing their mamas."

"Even now and then?" she asked.

I said, "Tee, she is just a mama like all of them. I'm living with her just now because I have to."

"But you could at least be nice to her."

What was this? I said, "I'm nice to her. I fill the wood boxes every day. Empty the ashes. Do a thousand things. I give her four dollars a month. What else can I do?"

"Don't you love her?" Tee asked.

My head shook in pure exasperation. How did she get on this subject? Feeling very uncomfortable with the whole trend of conversation, I got up and went around to the back of the house and split some wood, slamming the ax in.

Tee was too serious and womanly for me.

11

ONCE I WENT to a Manteo tent revival with Mama and sat on the front row with my feet in sawdust. During the preaching, the Reverend Peter Pender, imported from Gastonia, shouted into my face, "The devil's gotcha! You're goin' to hell!" He had red hair a shade lighter than Kilbie's and very sour breath. Why, I didn't even know that preacher; he'd never seen me until that night. But there have been times when I think he was right. I also think the Lord and the devil sometimes get together to undo a person.

On certain occasions, they seem to work hand in hand and leave human waste in the wake. However, I did not figure on *Him* and the devil teaming up in the weather department.

Not a full, raging nor'easter had hit us since December and one was overdue. From November until April, we usually averaged a big gale once a month. Winds and seas just as high as the afternoon the *Empress* plowed in.

Fates of one kind or another soon decided that the northeast wind would visit in the period of the new moon in February, informing ships at sea and coastal folks by barometers that fell slowly but surely. The needle told us that this wind would howl like it came from the icy backside of Hades, driving water over Diamond Shoals to treetop height; churning Wimble and Heron Head into a frenzy; mount waves of ten to twelve feet all along the Banks.

Big storms, not those pesky squalls that hit and run, send out their warning feelers and we began getting rain before first light opened. I filled the wood boxes after breakfast and tied off

Me and the John O'Neal to a scrub oak; then checked around to make sure there wasn't anything that would kite up against the house. I put some corn in a bucket in the shelter. Fid predicted as well as anybody what was coming and would soon leave the marsh to keep his shag partially dry. Boo Dog got ready to take his post on the hooked rug by the stove.

All the while I knew that the surfmen and keepers from Wash Woods, up by the Virginia border, on south, were checking equipment; looking out of their rain-spattered cupolas. Undoubtedly, on the previous sunset, with heavy clouds to north and east, they'd seen sails; plumes from steamers hull down on the horizon. The parade of ships by the Outer Banks never stopped although many were probably trying to hightail it to port this rainy morning.

Before noon, the first hard swipes of wind attacked the sand strips, gusting to forty knots; by noon, it was blowing steady, driving rain ahead of it with enough force to knife paint off bulkheads. The house vibrated and the myrtles and oaks, always bent west, bowed lower and hung to sand roots.

I took Tee to a special upright oak beam that Papa had sunk into the sand, lodging it on a big rock. It came up through the floor and went right to the roof. "Put your ear against it," I instructed. "You can feel the boom of the surf and hear it." I sometimes listened to it during storms—a crash every few seconds running up the grain of that old oak upright.

"Are we safe here?" Tee asked, slightly jumpy.

Mama called over. "This is jus' a gale o' wind. Not a hurrycane. We're safe as Boo's fleas. Only time to worry is when the water walks across the Banks. Even then, John O'Neal built this house to stay."

But as the afternoon wore on, Mama got the Bible out and read awhile. Not to beseech watch over us, however. Brother Reuben was on her mind, of a certainty. She asked, as usual, "Where do you think Reuben is today?"

"Safe in port in Trinidad," I said. I didn't know.

Tee and I played checkers after supper until it

was time to blow the lamps out. The house was dancing by then and the last thing I did before I went to bed was caulk the front doorjamb with burlap bags to keep wind from driving rain in.

Though it was still pelting, the worst of the gale was over when we woke up and by mid-morning, when Kilbie rode up, the wind was down to five knots or so. Banging water droplets off his sou'wester and rubber coat on the porch, he came on in to say, very soberly, "It's a bad one, Ben. I jus' come from the store. Four ships are wrecked. Closest one is between here an' Chicky. Filene's crew is out. Prochorus has his crew out; Cap'n Davis; Cap'n Etheridge; Cap'n Drink-water. Ever crew on the Banks is out, I expect . . ."

Kilbie was anxious to ride and wanted company.

I couldn't resist, as usual. The Chicky wreck wasn't that far away. I looked over at Tee. "You want to go? You'll see a sight."

Mama said peevishly, "Why, Ben? Why?" She was thinking Tee had already had her fill of storms and wrecks.

"It may be the only time she'll ever see a life-saving crew in action."

Mama sighed. "Why does she need to see it?"

I left the decision to Teetoncey. "I'd like very much to go," she told Mama. Well, who wouldn't? You name me a mainlander who wouldn't like to see a Hatteras wreck? Name me an exile from England who wouldn't like to see one.

So we dressed and I brought Fid out of the shelter and then we headed toward Chicky Station, riding double in the light rain; Kilbie slopping along beside on that slow old mule.

When we broke to the beach, surf roaring so loud we had to shout, the ocean stretched before us in mountains of white cresting water with foamy, gray valleys. Salt spray was heavy in the air, mist scooped from wavetops, still flying inland. For a mile offshore, the water was the color of bean soup from the boiling sand. Ever thus after a gale.

We rode on past Heron Head Station but didn't stop. No one was there, of course. Along with the lifesaving equipment, they were at the wreck, a little below Chicky Station. The Chicky boys were working a previous wreck to the north.

In another fifteen minutes, through the light rain, we picked up the vague shape of a ship near the beach; masts still up but rigging in a mess; hull still in one piece but probably already pounding apart. I judged it was about a hundred yards offshore. Kilbie said it had grounded about 9 A.M., a much better time to wreck than in pitch night.

Closer, we got a better look. "Three-masted schooner," I said to Tee.

The ship was sideways, parallel to the beach; breakers slamming against her starboard side. She was tilted over about twenty degrees. *Geraldine Solari, Brooklyn, New York*, was on her stern.

"Those men," Tee breathed, awed by it all, to my great satisfaction.

Yes, there were still some men aboard her, clinging midships along the port rail. The ship lifted and slammed against the bottom as each wave passed, shaking stem to stern.

As we reached the scene, Filene was getting ready to launch again. Four survivors were already huddled on the beach, staring anxiously out at their shipmates. "Filene'll save 'em all," I reassured Tee.

To those who have never watched a cedar-planked, oak-ribbed double-ended twenty-five-foot lifesaving boat go out through high surf, it is a moment beyond description. Papa once told Mama, "You feel like you're sitting on a half-hollow matchstick an' the breakers look like Smoky Mountain peaks."

Jabez and Mark Jennette were already in the heavy boat, cloaked in glistening oilskins, hooded under sou'westers, oars set to take the first sweep of storm water. Their faces were taut. Luther Gaskins, Jimmy Meekins, Malachi Gray, and Lem O'Neal, along with Keeper Midgett, were bending down to shove her full into the water, with Filene leaping aboard last to use his arms and back on the sweep oar, which would steer her.

We saw Filene watching the breakers, waiting

for the best one to roll in, then he bellowed, "Let's take her out," and the crew bent to shoot her into white water, leaping into their seats, grabbing oars, all in a molasses-smooth move.

Filene tumbled over the stern as Jabez and Mark heaved back mightily. The bow rose on froth and she speared toward the first big breaker.

The breakers were the killers and could make kindling of the thousand-pound boat, mangling every man aboard, in an eyeblink.

They rose on the first big one, climbing almost straight up.

We could hear Filene's hoarse yell—just a "Yaw——yaw——yaw" as he timed the oar strokes.

They crested it, spray flying, slamming over it, with ten feet of bow in sight; then buried in the wild trough of water and rose again to climb the next one.

Tee's mouth had dropped open and she was staring at the plunging boat, absolutely speechless.

The boat rose again on a hill of water, staggered a moment on the crest and I thought maybe Filene would broach, but then I saw that massive back literally swing the hull straight as it hung in air on the steering oar. In a moment, they were past the breaker line.

Tee said, "I never want to see that again." Under the brim of her sou'wester she was chalky. For mainlanders, maybe once is enough. But I reminded, "They got to come back, Teetoncey."

Filene steered to the portside of the schooner, the lee side, sheltered somewhat from the seas, and we watched as eight men went over the rail and into the pitching boat, one so weak he fell and almost went overboard. Then the boat pulled away for the return trip.

Kilbie said, "There's still one man aboard."

I looked closer. He sure was—by the foremast, and seemed to be clinging to it; not even offering himself for rescue.

Tee said anxiously, "They won't leave him, will they?"

"Never have," I answered. "They'll go back after him."

In a few minutes the survivors were safe on the beach without even getting their feet wet, and the crew was hauling the boat higher from the surf line.

"They're not going back out to get that man?" Tee asked worriedly, her voice squeaking.

I looked toward the schooner again, but Tee didn't really need to fret. Already Jabez and Lem O'Neal had the bronze Lyle gun in position; Jabez fixing the four-ounce powder charge and Lem getting the seventeen-pound ball shot and *shot line* ready.

"They'll take him off in the breeches buoy," I said, having some firsthand knowledge of that operation.

Staying well clear of the work, especially clear of Filene, I got close enough to Luther Gaskins to yell, "What's wrong with that man on the schooner?"

Busy readying lines and a big block, like a giant wooden pulley, Luther shouted back, "Two o' 'em out there. One's busted inside an' we don't want to try him in the boat. Chest is crushed. You can't see him from here. He's down on the deck."

In a few minutes, the Lyle gun boomed out, sending the ball shot over the bow of the ship. The strong, light No. 9 line was attached to it. Sometimes it took ten or twenty shots but Jabez was neat with this first one. The shot line was laying over the bow after riding down a mast stay and we saw the man fight his way forward up the slippery, slanting deck to grab it. Then he inched back with it and tied it off near the foremast.

I said, "Watch now." Next to surfboating, it was probably the best show on the Banks: Jabez and Lem O'Neal attached the heavy block to the light line. Through the block was reeved a *whip line,* a still heavier line to support the breeches buoy, the funny-looking canvas pants. Mark Jennette and Malachi Gray each got an end of the whipline as the man on board began to heave in.

Rain had stopped by now, and the wind had shifted around to west, helping to flatten the wavetops and push out the ebbing tide. Conditions couldn't have been better to watch a buoy rescue.

With Jennette and Malachi paying out slack, the sailor on the *Solari* dragged the heavy pulley and whip line out through the breakers. He finally pulled it over the side and then carried it back to the foremast, falling once on the sloping deck, skidding on his shoulders to the rail.

After tying it off tightly on the foremast, high up as he could reach, he waved. There was now a limp rope oval between ship and shore, running through the heavy block on the foremast. In a moment, the breeches buoy was dancing and flapping on its way toward the ship on the lower whip line.

We watched as the empty buoy wobbled in across the deck and then the sailor lifted the unconscious body and managed to slip the legs down through the holes.

Filene shouted, "Bring him home, boys," and four surfmen manned the whip line to return the buoy to shore with its injured cargo.

In another two minutes, he was gently lifted from the buoy while Tee turned her back, not wanting to see a man with a crushed chest.

The buoy was quickly returned to the wreck and the last survivor of the *Geraldine Solari* was soon safe onshore. In fact, all of them were on their way to Heron Head Station within a very short time. They'd have hot soup in their bellies and a drying out; then swap stories, as usual.

I was very glad that Teetoncey could see a Hatteras Banks rescue when it all went so smoothly and not a soul was lost.

We stayed on at the wreck for another three hours, helping the surfmen pull all manner of things from the water as the Brooklyn vessel broke up, mizzenmast shearing first.

Finally heading home about four o'clock, we saw someone approaching about a half mile from us on the seaward trail. Boo Dog began barking.

Soon, Mis' Mehaly Blodgett met us aboard her tackie and inquired as to where the keeper might be. I shushed Boo Dog down (he always barked at

Mis' Mehaly for reasons unknown), and pointed off toward what was left of the schooner. Most of Filene's crew was still there. "He's two miles off, Mis' Mehaly," I said.

The old woman, half deaf, almost toothless, yelled, "Ship's aground on Heron Head." Her one good eye was gleaming like a hazel jewel beneath her sou'wester brim.

Another wreck! It was hard to believe.

"You sure, Mis' Mehaly?" I asked.

"I'm sartain," she replied.

I still had my doubts. She couldn't see too well with that one eye, the other having been a victim to a fishhook when she was a child.

Kilbie said, "C'mon, let's go," and we charged off for Heron Head Shoal; Mis' Mehaly continuing on north to inform Filene.

As we bounced along, Tee asked, "Who was that?"

"Old woman from Buxton Woods, Mis' Mehaly Blodgett."

"She looks like a witch," said Tee.

She wasn't. Mama swore by her. She made the

best penetrates on the islands, adding sweet spirit of basil, orange peel, and lavender for tang. Her liver-sweeper was unique. Neither was there a better midwife than Mis' Mehaly. But it was very odd that she was this far north, out in the dregs of gale on mucky sand. Later, we asked her several times, but could never get a straight story and for a while Tee remained convinced she was a witch.

Reaching the beach at Heron about four-thirty, when a dozen rays of sun punched through cloud holes to west, I had the chill of my life. Tee gasped and Kilbie said, "Oh, Ben!"

Across the wintry sea, sitting in coffee-colored water at this period of low tide, *there was a ship*. But it was not a new wreck. Nothing from this storm.

We saw this: a skeleton of vessel, with some ribbing poking up, a donkey steam boiler with a short rusted stack; two splintered stubs of masts rising up about three feet. I could hardly breathe. Without doubt, it was the *Malta Empress*. Back from a voyage through sand.

The gale winds and rushing tide had shallowed out that bar, probably raised the hulk on high water; then let it lower to drop a skin of sand back over it, but not cover it completely. The bones of the *Empress* sat there, grim and gaunt, a dark, returned ship of the Hatteras ghost fleet.

A single sunbeam caught it, laying yellow on it against gray ocean, and we couldn't speak for a minute. It had to be the devil's work, but I was also certain the Lord had done this to me personally for failing to tell Mama about the bullion.

I thought Teetoncey was going to faint.

12

NEWS WENT the length of the Banks in no time at all. There was chittering and chattering and mule mounting. The wrecker blood was so thick in the Midgetts, the Farrows, the Gaskinses, the Gaskills, the Gillikins, and I suppose one O'Neal, at least, that people could smell a resurfaced hulk over and above the fish frying at suppertime. They started to come before the first star was out.

Frank Scarborough joined us just after dark, whispering, "Anybody know 'bout the bullion?"

I shook my head hard enough to warn him to shut up. Then we younguns gathered driftwood to get a bonfire going. Jabez spilled some coal oil from a lantern to help the wet wood ignite. The whole Heron Head crew was there, but none of them had seen what was on the bar. Night had fallen before they could arrive after working the *Solari* wreck.

Although the tide was coming in strongly again, Filene wanted to launch; go out and take a look around. Low water would be about six in the morning and they could get a better look then, but Filene wouldn't put it off. The keeper didn't quite believe Mis' Mehaly, nor Kilbie and myself. He wouldn't even believe Tee. Yet he couldn't contain his curiosity.

For one, I was happy that he was about to row out; not delay. From the looks of it, the *Empress* had raised herself about six feet but that wouldn't be enough to expose the chests. Her keel was still covered with sand. If the chests had bobbed up, we'd just all act surprised.

Teetoncey's mood had changed. Her eyes

were distant, and she hardly said a word; wouldn't even look out toward the shoal. She just stood around, her thoughts somewhere else, and no one paid much attention to her, including me.

Warming his meaty hands, the keeper was near the bonfire, burning blue red because of the salt in the wood. I did hear him say to Luther Gaskins, "If it is the *Empress,* somehow I wish she'd never surfaced. That ship is beginnin' to hant me." Few things ever haunted Filene, but if he'd seen her at yellow sunset it might have happened. He would have run for his Bible.

However, some people on the Banks did believe that a ship come back from a voyage in the sand was bad luck for us all. I did not agree. What could have been luckier than to have this particular barkentine pop up?

A few minutes later, the surf crew launched and we all moved closer to the waterline to watch them pull out. Only Tee stayed by the fire, staring into it; a small figure dwarfed by my old rubber coat. I yelled for her to come on but she shook her head. Surely, the sight of the ghost hulk had unnerved her. I hoped her nerves weren't shot to the point of confession.

There really wasn't much to see at that. The night was black as deck tar and the boat disappeared into it. We followed the lantern that Filene was holding as it bobbed over the choppy sea.

Frank got me to one side worriedly. "Maybe they'll find the chests?"

That was silly. Filene couldn't have seen his own boots out there unless he held the lantern over them. The tide was already lapping across the shoal. The only thing they could do was to make certain it was the *Empress* hulk. In the morning would be the anxious time. They might spot something then.

Soon, we saw the lantern turn parallel to the beach, so we knew they were going along the sandbar, Filene trying to get a good look. Then the boat stopped a moment, and Kilbie said quietly, "That's bad."

We could see the keeper waving the lantern back and forth, likely scanning what was visible of the boiler stack and mast stubs. Finally, his shout fought its way back through the westerly breeze. "It's her!"

That was certainly no surprise to Kilbie and myself. Absolutely it was the British bark. But everyone else whooped it up. There were about fifty people, mostly from Chicky but some from Clarks. They all yelled or said something excitable. It wasn't often that a wreck surfaced. But they only knew the half.

I went back to the fire and said to Teetoncey, "Filene knows we weren't jesting."

She passed over that to ask, "Can we go home, Ben?"

"What's wrong?"

"I'm not feeling very well." Her wan look verified that statement.

"Just as soon as Filene gets back," I promised. Right then, I wouldn't have left the beach for a round-trip ticket to New York City via railroad sleeping car.

The boat returned to shore about seven o'clock and the crew piled out, not saying much.

Wrecks, even old ones, did that to them occasionally. Filene moved forward and then stepped out on the beach. I tightened up, wondering if he'd mention the chests. All he said was, "It's been a long day. Why don't you folks go home an' git some supper."

Frank Scarborough's papa asked, "What'd you see, Filene?"

The lantern glow plainly showed that the keeper wasn't up to a lot of talk. He muttered, "We seen a hulk that killed thirteen people."

I heard Tee make a small noise.

Then Filene looked back out at the bar, shaking his head.

Jabez broke the silence. "Boys, let's secure the boat till mornin'." They pulled it high on the beach.

Everyone went to their houses, including Tee and myself. The Hatteras cat had her tongue all the way home though I tried to make her talk; telling her how we could get that silver in a snap.

Naturally, Mama wasn't at all pleased with the discovery that Mis' Mehaly had made. She said,

"Remains o' humans an' ships should be left in peace."

I said, "The wind and sea did it. Mis' Mehaly didn't."

Mama answered gloomily, "It bodes no good, Ben," and went about serving supper, thinking her mystical thoughts about the sea.

I woke up before dawn but later than I'd planned, dressed hurriedly, and then went in to shake Tee. Her eyes were closed but I don't think she'd been asleep. I doubt she'd slept at all during the night. I whispered, "Get dressed and let's go."

She whispered back, "I don't want to, Ben. I'm not going out there again."

Now we had two females in the house who were skitterish of that ocean. I said, "C'mon, Tee. Filene'll launch soon. He may see something this morning."

"I'm not going," she whispered fiercely.

Puzzled, I shrugged and went on out. Mama would be delighted that she stayed home, but how she could sprawl there knowing that the surfmen might spot those chests was beyond me. Even if that ship hadn't had a red cent aboard I would have gone.

Filene was already at sea when I arrived at Heron Shoal about seven o'clock. The sun wasn't up but there was plenty of gray light. A half dozen people had beat me to the scene. I said "Hello" to Mr. Burrus.

"That gives me the willies," he said, nodding toward the bar.

Much more of the *Empress* could be seen this morning, though her keel was still well down in sand. Short pieces of ribbing cupped up like brown bent fingers. The sea must have sliced her about six or eight feet above the keel, swept everything off her except the stubs of curved ribs; the donkey boiler and nubs of busted masts.

"Looks like a giant fish cleaved above the backbone, don't it?" said Mr. Burrus.

She did, a little. Like a fish skeleton that had parked on the beach for years, parted with its meat, head, and tail; showing only its bones. But these were dirty brown instead of sun parched.

Filene had anchored to the shoal and all the crew were leaning over the side to study the hulk. Then, suddenly, there seemed to be excitement in the boat. They'd spotted something. My heart sank to my toenails.

I couldn't recognize who it was, but one of the surfmen took an oar and began pushing the blade into the sand; then it looked like Malachi Gray getting out on the bar. Then Filene and Jabez climbed out. All three knelt down and seemed to be scraping sand.

I was beside myself.

Hardie Miller shouted out, "What do you see, Filene?"

The keeper paid us no mind although I don't think he could hear Hardie across eight hundred yards and over surf noise.

Feeling low, not even believing myself, I said to Mr. Burrus, "I bet they don't find anything."

Just then Kilbie came up on foot and I ran over to him. "Damnation," I said. "I think they found them."

Kilbie squinted toward the bar. "They're not in the right position, Ben."

"You hope," I whispered.

"They ought to be by that mainmast stub," said Kilbie.

"Well, don't suggest it."

Filene and his men fooled around on that bar for almost an hour while Kilbie and I went daft on the beach. Hardie even got so mad at the keeper that he threatened to go back to Big Kinnakeet and haul his skiff up and go out and take a look himself. If he'd known bullion was on that bar, he would have swum out in the winter sea. Hardie was a dedicated wrecker.

Finally, about eight, when the tide had well covered the bar again, the Heron Head surfmen returned to the beach. No sooner had the prow touched when Mr. Burrus asked, "What'd you see?"

"Nothin' but a broken cask," said Filene. "Let that hulk rest in peace."

Kilbie and I almost sagged to the sand in relief.

Now, we had a clear shot ahead unless some big mouth cut loose. That nor'easter had practically done all the work for us, digging more sand away than two steam shovels could have. If we burrowed down two feet we'd have the bullion. And from now on, nobody would pay much attention to that wreck.

If the weather was favorable we planned to go out three days hence. I talked to Tee about it but she wanted no part. Well, that was just as good. It would be quicker and easier with just three of us.

For two days, one of us kept an eye on the wreck and on the beach. Curiosity had died down and by the end of the second day, no one went off the trail to even peek at the *Empress* hulk.

I had a problem at home, though. Mama would likely spot the empty sawhorses that had been holding *Me and the John O'Neal*. I finally figured out what to do. Morning of the second day, I tossed an old tarpaulin over it, so the shape was outlined. Then that night I went out and quickly dragged the boat about eighty feet away, hiding it in the brush. Then I laid some planks over the sawhorses; built up a shape of a boat with more brush; then covered it with the tarp. From the kitchen window it would look like the boat was still there. The Widow O'Neal would never know the difference until we'd returned it, along with a hundred thousand in bullion.

Kilbie had figured out just about what time the Heron Head patrol might pass, and we'd have about an hour, which is all the tide would allow us, anyway. But with three shovels working, we could dig out two feet of sand in ten minutes, heave those chests up separately, and be on our way.

Thursday afternoon found us hiding behind a dune, boat with us, as Jimmy Meekins plodded north on that leg of his patrol. We let him get about a mile up the beach, and then I said, "Let's launch and be quick about it."

Shovels, long probe, and anchor in it, we pulled the boat down to the surf, and in no time I was rowing out to the *Empress*.

Kilbie said, "We shouldn't have too much trouble now that she's this high."

I didn't think so, either.

From the looks of her, scanning from the

beach, the *Empress* hadn't moved an inch. The tide was almost out; very little breeze and the ocean was calm.

I laid my back into the oars and I don't think it took us more than four or five minutes to reach the bar. Kilbie heaved the anchor up on it, and we got out in a hurry, moving the shovels and probe up near the stub of mainmast.

Frank stopped a minute, though. "I don't like it out here," he said.

Kilbie and I weren't exactly thrilled. The stubs of ribs, covered with small barnacles, were dripping; there was some Gulf Stream seaweed draped over the rusted stack of the boiler, tiny crabs weaving in and out of it.

"Start shoveling, and we'll get off," I said, having no time to waste on how the hulk looked.

Kilbie walked back about six feet from the mainmast and said, "Let's try here."

We all started to shovel and in a few minutes, Frank said, "I hit something. But it's soft."

"Keep digging," I said.

Sand was plopping around.

"What is this?" Kilbie asked, as we uncovered more of something. It was like a hunched bundle of cloth.

"Whatever it is, let's get it out," I said, getting nervous about the tide coming in again. "Chests may be under it."

All of a sudden, Frank yelled, "Gawd!" but not without some reverence. He dropped his shovel.

We'd uncovered a body!

Frank said, "I think I'm gonna be sick," and went to the other end of the bar.

Of all the rotten luck!

I said, "What do we do now?"

Kilbie replied, "Let's get him out of here. Can't leave him."

I wanted to know why not. He was useless.

"I think it would be against the law," said Kilbie.

We turned him over. He was like a mummy. I took a look at his face and then quickly looked away. It was all shriveled, like a prune.

But Kilbie took a long look. That boy had the spirit of a mortician. He said thoughtfully, "The cold, wet sand preserved him, Ben."

I did not give one good damn about the sand preserving him.

Kilbie went on, "The fish an' crabs didn't get to him. He's jus' puckered up an' gray, like your fingers if you hold 'em underwater. He's the color o' slate an' his eyes have a film on them. He's not bloated at all."

Refusing to look at him, I said, "Let's roll him off the shoal."

"He's gonna float," Kilbie replied. "We better take him back ashore. Either that or anchor him."

"I'm not losing my anchor on him," I said. If we'd had a *killick,* which is a hunk of stone used for an anchor, I wouldn't have minded. But I'd searched high and low for my iron anchor and it was valuable.

Kilbie said, "Ben, we got to take this man back ashore an' be legal. Anybody finds out, an' we could spend the rest o' our days in state jail in Raleigh."

I sighed. "All right."

There went the salvage work for this day.

I yelled over to Frank. "Come on, an' help us."

He was puking.

So Kilbie and I dragged that shrunken, gray-puckered sailor over to the boat and dumped him in. Maybe Mama was right. That hulk bode no good. And now someone could think about digging a fourteenth grave for the *Empress* people over by Chicky.

I'm telling you that that wreck was defying us something awful. It was out there to be salvaged and every which way we turned we were defeated. The tide was already coming back. The only thing to do was go to the beach, hide the boat, and then notify the station that a body had drifted up out of the barkentine, and washed ashore.

We got ready to shove off, and I said to Frank, disappointed in him, "Get in this boat now or stay here all night."

Green as summer collards, he got in, casting glassy eyes up at the sky instead of down in the bilge where that sopping, sandy bundle was.

Kilbie pushed us out and I began to row toward shore.

Much to our sorrow, Luther Gaskins had never told us that he saw us that first day when I dumped the boat. It had not occurred to either Kilbie or myself that we could easily be seen from the Heron Head Station lookout. Worse still, Lem O'Neal had flu that day and Keeper Midgett took his postnoon watch.

With his long glass, Filene always scanned everything in the ocean, be it birds or flopping fish or broom handles or boats and ships. I can only imagine his grunt when he focused in on us. He then got Jabez to relieve him, mounted his tackie, and went south.

No sooner had I brought the *Me and the John O'Neal* beautifully through the surf when that old crone of a man stood up behind the dune where he'd been hiding and shouted down, "Whatcha got, boys?"

13

ALTHOUGH MY COUSIN Filene occasionally performed like a jackass, to quote Mama, he was not an ignorant peasant. He looked at the three of us to judge the weakest and selected Frank Scarborough, whose face was just as gray and almost as puckered as the corpse in the boat.

Filene roared at Frank, "What were you doin' out there?"

"Lookin' for the silver," Frank blabbed.

K. B. Oden and myself could have gladly hit him with a postie.

"What silver?" Filene shouted.

Frank's lower lip was quivering. "The hundred thousand that's on the *Empress*."

Filene just *harrumph*ed and dropped his eyes to the bundle in the bottom of my boat. "An' you found a dead man?"

"Yes, Cap'n," said Frank, about to be sick again.

(Kilbie and I never had much respect for Frank after that time.)

Keeper Midgett took one of my oars and turned the dead man over, prompting Frank to go "Ooooooohhhattttttt" and run down the beach.

I looked away myself.

The next afternoon, I felt like I was on trial. Mama, Teetoncey, Kilbie, Frank, and myself all sat in the messroom of Heron Head Station with Filene Midgett acting like a magistrate.

He addressed himself to Teetoncey. "Is what I heerd true? I frankly didn't believe it, not with these boys involved." He wagged his head at us.

She nodded.

"You mean there is twenty thousand pounds o' silver on that shoal? A hundred thousand dollars?"

She nodded again.

Filene cleared his throat. "Miss, I never question the truth, but this time I . . ."

Tee interrupted. "It is true, Captain."

Despite his official position, old wrecker blood charged up through Filene's veins and his eyes grew to the size of muskenong grapes and then went back to pinpoints. "Rachel," he said, "I'm ashamed o' you for not tellin' me."

Mama bristled. "I did not know a thing till last night. The time before, I thought they were jus' foolin' aroun' out on that bar."

They all looked at me as if it was totally my fault.

In fact, Filene gazed long at me. "You any ideer what's gonna happen? Word'll be all over by nightfall. Ever fool for five hundred miles'll start thinkin' about ways to git that bullion. Ever criminal from Baltimore south'll be packin' his kit within a week. Top o' that, the British consul, a man I dislike, will surely lay claim for Her Majesty."

I thought: And you can bet the greedy U.S.A. government will try to scoop up a big chunk just to run the Post Office department. I had given up hope of shares myself but dared to ask, "What about Teetoncey here? It was her papa's money."

For a second, the O'Neals were united. Mama chimed up, "Yes, what about Teetoncey?"

Filene stared at us. "Maritime laws govern salvage. You know that, Rachel."

Already, they were planning to rob Teetoncey of her rightful money and it was sure that Uncle Salisbury would be packing his own bag to get aboard the *Lucania*. Greed was everywhere.

Filene got back to me. "What'd you see out there, Ben?"

With all our plans definitely gone to seed, I looked at Mama; then at Kilbie, Frank, and Tee. There wasn't any use to withhold information. Old Filene would likely be nosing around by dusk. "We saw nothing that you didn't see, Cap'n. But Kilbie thinks he knows the location of the silver."

Filene glanced at Kilbie, going "Umh-huh, umh-huh." He scratched his close-cropped head, maybe fighting off the inclination to go out and do a little personal salvage work himself. "Where, Kilbie?"

"A few feet back from the mainmast," Kilbie answered. "Tee said her papa strapped 'em off to the mainmast where it entered the cabin deck."

"I see," Filene said, many thoughts probably turning over under that prickly gray scalp.

Mama asked insistently, "Filene, who does own that silver?"

"That's a difficult question. First, we'll have to determine if it was on the manifest, providin' the Barbadoes has a copy. If it wasn't, Teetoncey's papa was doin' a lil' smuggling . . ."

Tee gasped and Mama said sharply, "Watch your tongue, Filene."

The keeper countered, "Rachel, we've had three ships to my knowledge that carried gold or silver without listin' it. I'm bringin' up the possibility."

Mama huffed. "Well, jus' don't bring it up till your facts are clear, an' you still haven't answered my question. Who owns that silver?"

"It's very tricky, Rachel. We'll jus' have to let the law decide . . ."

Fare thee well, Teetoncey's rightful money, I thought.

Mama took a deep breath. "As this is a time for confession, Filene, I must tell you that Teetoncey *does* have relatives in London."

He blinked at the castaway girl.

"I didn't tell you partly because I wanted her to stay; partly because she didn't want to go."

Filene laughed with misery. "I'll sure be glad when this winter's over." He shook his head. "Well, I guess I'll have to truck with that consul again, though someone else can board him this time. That man'll never set foot in my command again."

"I'm glad you know," Mama said, having taken a weight off her mind.

Filene dismissed us with a caution to stay off the shoal, keep our mouths shut, and hang on to our straps. Then Mama gave him a word of caution. "Don't you go spreadin' word about Mr. Appleton till you know your facts."

The keeper just sighed.

On the way home I was not at all surprised to hear that Methodist woman say, "Money is the blight o' the earth."

Feeling low, Tee and I walked over to Heron Head at sunset. I told her a dozen times that Filene was just talking through his hat when he mentioned smuggling but she was still hurting. Mama said that Filene had lost control of himself because he was the last to mention the dead in any disgraceful way. I think so, too.

There must have been two hundred people on the beach just looking out at some white water curling over top a sandbar, from which rib members and a metal pipe projected. Nobody was saying much and they all acted quite cool to me. Frank's papa was there and gave me a very fishy eye. The Gillikins were there and you would have thought Tee and I had *ague*.

But it was Mis' Hazel Burrus who actually said it. "Were you an' your mama takin' care o' Tee-toncey jus' to git that silver?"

I couldn't believe it. We'd been friends with all

these people for fifty years. Some were kin. Hazel Burrus was a Bible reader with Mama. Yet they now suspected us of skulduggery.

The men were closer down to the water, some huddled in groups, talking in low voices; now and then looking out at Heron bar. Hardie Miller said to me, "Ben, you broke a wrecker law on these Banks. You tried to keep it all for yourself . . ." Talk about honesty! Hardie had about as many scruples as a hammerhead shark.

I felt hot tears near my eyelids and quickly went back up the dune where Filene was sitting, having his evening pipe. He'd been hearing this nasty talk from other people and said a nice thing to me. "Ben, you'll be mommicked an' in storms the rest o' your life. Learn to ride 'em out."

Teetoncey and I fled toward home.

There was some gloom over the O'Neal house that night but Mama tried to be cheerful. She was never one to hold grudges nor to let her anger do more than quickly pass through her craw. I told her what had happened down on the beach and she said, "They'll sleep on it, Ben.

An' after calm daylight, they'll decide we're noble people after all."

We sat around after supper and talked awhile. Though I wish she hadn't, Mama declared that she thought one reason the *Empress* was lost was simply because of all that bullion on board. Weight had nothing to do with it. The silver itself had doomed the bark.

I saw Tee thinking seriously about it.

We were all down in the mouth and that mystical story went with that condition.

Part of the gloom, of course, was the knowledge that Teetoncey would leave us soon, now that the consul had been notified she had London relatives. I was actually growing to like her. She was sure different from Banks girls. In that hairpin body was a lot of spunk.

The subject was only brought up once that night and Mama commented, though she was brokenhearted, "We'll wait an' see. But, Teetoncey, you might even like to git back to England. To that nice, big house. Go to those fancy dress shops, eat your own kind o' food. You might even find yourself takin' to that uncle an' his younguns."

Tee seemed resigned now. "I hope," she said.

The next week was difficult. I worked twice at the Burrus store but not a soul that came in mentioned Heron Head or Teetoncey. Mis' Burrus continued cool, and I couldn't have cared less. She was a turncoat. Mr. Burrus was himself, though he didn't say a word about the *Empress* fortune and everything that had happened.

Time to time we heard things. The surfmen were keeping people away from the shore, as best they could, and Filene crewed his boat to row out and chase a sloop that had sailed from Norfolk for a bit of salvage work. Outlanders were beginning to show up and the keeper was more afraid they'd drown than find the bullion. He didn't want his record blemished any more than it was.

The consul, we'd heard by then, was waiting instructions from London and even with those steamships making a crossing in six or seven days, mail took three weeks to reach Norfolk.

Even if Tee's uncle was headed toward us, it would still be mid or late March before she left.

Teetoncey was with me a lot those days, doing some of the things we'd done when she was in her catatonic state. Foolish things like shouting up and down the steps of Hatteras Light; going to watch the snow geese on Pea Island. I must say it was an improvement over previous weeks. I was exhausted from fighting the battles of hiding her and hunting the fortune in silver.

She *was* different. Imagine anybody finding beauty in driftwood. She did. She held up a gnarled piece of satiny gray wood and said, "Ben, this is breathtaking." There was enough of it on the Banks to let her hold her breath a thousand years.

Tee was moody the afternoon we went up to watch the snow geese. She sat on the flats, her elbows upon her knees, just staring at the geese as they flapped and moved about, making a lot of noise.

Suddenly she asked, "Ben, will you come and see me in London? After you start going to sea?"

"If I get over that way," I said.

"I'd like that. I could show you a lot of things. We could go to exciting places together."

That would be fine, I thought, in case I ever got to London. I did want to see some of the trains, those roof-seat buses, and that tunnel under the Thames River. I couldn't figure out how they did that. How do you bore through mud? Only worms had been successful thus far.

"It might be a couple of years," I said.

"I'll wait," Teetoncey answered, looking over at me. Her yellow hair was poking out from under the red bob-cap. She looked prettier than ever. She leaned over, kissed my cheek, and got up quickly to walk to the pony cart.

I sat there with my face feeling like I'd dipped it into hot embers.

14

FILENE CAME OVER two days later and confirmed what we'd heard: A man named Harkness and one named Beatty, from up on Roanoke Island, had sailed out of Oregon Inlet; come down to Heron Shoal a night past for a little digging. Harkness had drowned.

There were now fifteen casualties because of the *Malta Empress*. Enough, it would seem, to satisfy the ocean. Yet, not quite.

"Though the best tide is still a few days away, we can't wait any longer, Rachel. We'll have more graves on these Banks than there is sand. No matter how we warn people, they're gonna try to take that bullion."

Mama asked, "When'll you do it?"

"Day after tomorry. I've notified the assistant inspector an' he notified the consul. They're on their way."

"I'm sure glad, Filene. We should all git this behind us." At last, they were joined in mind.

He nodded agreement, then said, "I been studyin' salvage laws, Rachel. This is complicated an' I jus' don't know how it'll work out but if Teetoncey here is to share anythin', she best be on that barge with us. Mebbe even stick a shovel in. She's the owner's representative."

I looked over at Tee. She'd closed her eyes from the very thought of any salvage.

"Miss, you don't have to go," Filene said quickly. "I'm jus' tellin' what I think. I don't even know I'm right."

Mama offered, "I'll go out with you, Tee."

That was truly astonishing. Mama hadn't been on the ocean since John O'Neal's boat capsized.

She'd sworn she'd never go on it again. It was Sodom and Gomorrah to her. Besides, she had a terrible cold.

"Do what you think is best," said Filene, and departed.

Now, there is nothing trickier than maritime salvage laws. It takes a hogpen full of lawyers just to figure out who gets what and why. It would seem just and fair that Teetoncey would be the sole owner of whatever money her papa had carried up from the Barbadoes. Not so. To claim it all, she'd have to sit on that bar, and then have the money to hire a salvage crew, and then guard it with her life. Those things accomplished, the state government, claiming water rights to mean high tide, and bottom rights for some distance to sea, would try to lay an open palm in; then the fat, greedy federal government would twist the law to see how much it could steal from both the state of North Carolina and Teetoncey, as well as everyone else. Government theft seems to be legitimate.

I went over to Heron Head Station to find out

how Filene planned to raise the chests. Locating Jabez, he told me, "We're puttin' a rig on the *Beulah* today so we can lift 'em out with a block an' taykle. Shovel out first an' then put a hitch on 'em."

The *Shallowbag Beulah* was an old, beat-up, mud-spattered work barge down from Shallowbag Bay, in Manteo, anchored just inside Oregon Inlet, on the Pamlico. Flat-bottom and clumsy, it was about forty feet in length, twelve or so wide. Some government men had used it for surveying the past two summers. We'd played on it when it was anchored off Chicky village. Diving from it; crabbing off it with rotten fishheads for bait. I'd gotten a bad splinter from it in my right big toe. I knew the *Beulah*.

Jabez went on, "Luther an' Mark are up there now doin' the riggin'. Puttin' up two oak beams for standin' cargo booms. Whole crew'll take a boat tonight on the wagon an' then we'll tow the *Beulah* around beginnin' at daybreak. Anchor her good an' then do it day after tomorry."

I thought that was a little better plan than Kilbie had.

"We'll use about thirty shovelers an' they're drawin' lots for 'em tonight at the Burrus store. Filene still don't know they'll git any share but he's doin' it anyhow . . ."

Jabez laughed. "Alriddy, I heerd rumors these men'll share five hundred dollars each. No truth to that. But mebbe they will. Mebbe they won't. Filene says the courts'll decide."

I said, "It's a funny thing. Everybody's forgotten that the money really belongs to Teetoncey."

The chinless surfman nodded soberly. "Yes, they have. What's more, they've lost sight it might not be sittin' on that keel. You thought about that?"

I said I had. It would serve them right.

However, I still felt obliged to be on that barge or shoveling sand on that shoal when those chests came up, if they did.

I sought out Filene and pled guilty to numerous sins over the past month but then requested, "Cap'n, let me go out. I swear I'll do exactly what you say. Anything you say."

He answered sympathetically. "Ben, men are drawin' lots for a place on that barge."

"I won't ask to share," I promised. "Mama and Tee'll be on there. I got to go. We're family, after all."

He considered it a moment, then said, "All right, Ben. When I say sit you sit; when I say stand you stand . . ."

That didn't change a solitary thing. More or less, I'd been doing that for Filene since Papa died.

"I promise," I said.

The day for salvage on Heron Head Shoal was chilly and damp, even raw, as colorless as an oyster. But the wind was light and sea conditions favorable. Unless the weather shifted suddenly, there was no reason not to skim that bar in much less than an hour. With thirty shovelers, it wouldn't take long to heave sand and leave the *Malta Empress* cleaner than a holiday hen.

Mama's cold was still plaguing her. She was coughing pretty badly. She took a Mehaly penetrate around noon and then bundled up in a sweater and oilskin coat; shawl to protect her ears. Tee got dressed for chill weather, too. I'd been ready to go since early morning.

Tee wasn't very happy about going to the barge. Neither was Mama. But rather than have her lose everything, it was a chore to be done. Like pulling a troublesome tooth.

About one o'clock, I hitched Fid to the pony cart and we started off, Boo riding in back; Tee with the reins, as she now liked that assignment.

As we came over the final dune, Mama muttered, "I cannot believe it!"

There must have been five hundred people on the beach, mostly Bankers but a lot of mainlanders. As we got closer, I saw the British consul; Inspector Timmons; the wreck commissioner, and some other men I'd never seen before.

The barge was already anchored at the east lip of the shoal. Two surfboats were ready for launching from the beach. Filene's crew was there; so was Cap'n Davis's crew from Chicky.

We parked Fid and went on over.

Kilbie, fit to be tied because he couldn't go out, said, "It looks like a circus."

That it did.

The British consul came up to us and tipped

his derby. He greeted Mama and she answered on the cool side. He said to Teetoncey, "We've met before, young lady, but you probably don't remember. I'm Consul Calderham." He looked a lot better than the last time I saw him.

Tee gave him a slight formal bow and said, "How do you do." So British.

Calderham said, "You'll be happy to know that it won't be long until we have you returned safely to England. Away from this rustic place. I'm awaiting word from your uncle."

Tee said, "Thank you, sir."

Mama said to the consul, "Watch out you don't step in that fresh mule dung."

He looked down at his shoes and by the time he looked up we were moving on.

"I don't like him," said Tee instantly.

"That makes a hundred of us," Mama replied.

When we got to the Heron Head boat, Mama asked Filene, "Who are all these people?" She nodded toward the mainlanders, those she didn't know.

Filene laughed. "Well, that one's from the

U.S.A. Treasury; that's a state taxman; that's a county taxman. I'm surprised Congress isn't here today."

"Trash fish all," Mama muttered, and coughed hard. There wasn't much less distinction that could be applied to anything.

I looked out at the barge. It seemed to be all set. They'd rigged those oak beams in an upside-down V with the block and tackle dropping down from the point. Six or eight men could pull on the purchase line, the lifting line, and yank those chests out with no trouble.

Mama said to Filene, "Cousin, I jus' hope we don't find nothin' but sand an' shells."

Just about that time, the federal man walked up to Filene, dressed fancily. He said, "Keeper, I'll lay claim to those chests just as soon as you get them on shore."

Filene answered respectfully, "Yessir, but the state man has said he's layin' claim."

"You're a federal employee, aren't you?"

Filene answered, "Yessir. All I plan to do is turn 'em over to Inspector Timmons." That was neat passing of responsibility if I'd ever over-heard it.

Mama shook her head and walked away.

I saw her talking earnestly to Teetoncey but didn't think much about it. Those two were al-ways nose to jowl now, plotting something with dresses or doilies.

Shovels were being tossed into the Chicky boat. The tide would be below the bar in another half hour. Then Cap'n Davis shoved his boat off with the first load.

A few minutes later we got set to load into Filene's boat. He would row shorthanded to ac-commodate more people. The sea was practically flat.

Just before gathering her skirts up to step in, Mama looked at me with resignation. She said, "Ben, I swore I'd never go out again. And after this day, I won't."

Then I helped Tee in and climbed in myself. About ten or twelve shovelers—Farrows, Scar-boroughs, Millers, Gillikins, even Mr. Burrus—threw a leg in and sat down.

Jabez, Luther, Malachi, and Mark rowed us

out, with Filene steering. We went out in a hurry and I didn't hear a word said, as if we were hunting wild gobblers west of Mattamuskeet, stealthily sneaking through brush. Everyone was staring toward the *Empress,* entranced and thinking of money.

Tee sat beside me.

I whispered, "It won't take long, and we'll be back on shore."

Her head bobbed in a slight nod. Her lips were tight, though.

As I'd heard it, they planned to beach the barge after towing it ashore, drop the chests to ground; then they'd go by wagon to whoever got grubby hands on them. It sure wouldn't be Wendy Lynn Appleton.

Coming alongside the stern of the barge and tying up, Filene helped Mama aboard; then I gave Teetoncey a boost, and got up myself. Then the shovelers came aboard. The barge was lodged right up on the bar; the block and tackle hanging down toward the sand. There was still about an inch of water over the shoal.

Mama and Tee stayed near the stern, sitting

down next to each other on a fish box, Mama pulling the shawl tighter around her head to ward off the cold air.

I went forward to where most of the men were swinging down, shovels in hand. They began slopping around the shoal and looking at the hulk. Filene said to them, "Another ten minutes an' then let's dig that keel clean. Start right by the mainmast."

I noticed that Hardie Miller went straight to that spot as if he thought he might get an extra share if his shovel tapped a chest first.

Jabez stood beside me, looking down. "We're all gonna feel pretty foolish if there's nothing there."

The water fell rapidly and in another few minutes there were only a half dozen small pools left on Heron Shoal. Filene shouted, "Dig out," and thirty shovels bit into sand.

The keeper called back to Teetoncey. "Miss, I think you should go down an' dig a few shovels jus' for legal purpose."

She came forward slowly.

"You want me to go with you?"

"Please, Ben," she answered.

Filene lowered her down and I jumped down, too. He passed a shovel and Tee began to half-heartedly dig, just tossing small scoops back into the ocean.

Mama had come to the bow and was looking down at all of us. Sand was flying all over the place. She shook her head and returned to the stern.

I would guess that ten tons of sand and slime water was moved on that bar in less than twenty minutes. Men were getting sand on their faces, on their hats, and in the tops of their boots. Nobody was speaking to each other. Just digging. Wild-eyed.

Tee stopped. "I can't," she said. She was standing practically on the spot where she'd been in the cabin with her mama and papa.

As Filene was helping her back aboard the barge, there was a shout from Cletus Gillikin who was more toward the stern of the hulk. "I got somethin', Filene."

A dozen men converged and I ran toward the spot. Sand and water flew. In a few seconds, we saw two chests, tied together. Shouts rose from the bar and they were echoed on the beach.

Filene ordered the barge to be moved. Malachi Gray, along with Mark, ran to pull the two anchors that had her locked to the shoal. Then a dozen men pushed her maybe twenty feet broadside up the bar, opposite the hole.

I joined them.

Teetoncey was standing on the bow and looking down at the chests.

Filene asked, "Those the ones?"

She nodded and then walked aft, as if she didn't care a thing in the world about them.

Two or three men grabbed new line and worked it around the chests while others shoveled frantically to keep the wet slime from covering them.

Filene shouted, "I need three or four men up here to heave in."

Jabez was already on the purchase line, waiting.

The men scrambled aboard and began to heave.

The heavy chests came slowly out of the sand with a sucking noise, and then the shovelers left on the bar helped ease them across until they were directly under the bow of the *Beulah*.

There wasn't too much time to spare. Slack water was over and in another ten minutes the shoal would be visited with a fresh tide.

Soon, the two bullion chests dangled from the bow of the *Shallowbag Beulah* and Filene yelled for everyone to get aboard.

I clambered back up, along with all the shovelers. They were talking now, all right. Chittering and chattering; jabbering, speculating just how much this twenty minutes of shoveling would add to their pockets.

I took a good look at the locked chests. They were brass bound as Tee had said; the wood was dark from waterlogging. That wouldn't hurt the silver, of course. It was hard to believe. A hundred thousand dollars hung in the air from the bow of the *Beulah*.

Filene yelled, "All right, let's head for the beach."

Cap'n Davis promptly got his crew into the Chicky boat; Filene's crew climbed into the Heron Head boat, and then they drifted off forty or fifty feet to begin the tow to shore in tandem.

Filene shouted again: "Cast off when you're ready."

Several of the men pulled the anchors up and we were free of Heron Head. The two boat crews bent to oars and we started heading seaward. Soon, we'd turn and go south along the shoal and then angle in toward shore, taking advantage of the southing current.

From the beach, it must have been quite a picture: the *Beulah,* loaded with people, a fortune in bullion dangling from the bow, being towed by two surfboats manned with oarsmen.

All the men were standing near the chests like two-legged vultures, just yapping happily, and I stood there myself for a while, vulture like the rest. Then I went to the stern, where Mama and Tee were seated on the fish box.

Mama asked, "Ben, how much water we in?" She coughed and drew the oilskins closer around her throat.

I looked down over the side. We were now about seven hundred yards away from the shoal, seaward, and I'd always heard there was ninety to a hundred feet in this spot. "Ninety, hundred feet," I said.

Mama asked Teetoncey a strange question. "You've thought it all over again? Last time, Tee."

Tee said, "Please, Mrs. O'Neal."

I was puzzled when Mama got up and started walking forward. I'd noticed she'd brought a big canvas drawstring bag with her but didn't know why. I thought maybe she'd brought some crochet work out, although Atlantic swells weren't the place to do that.

I followed as Mama walked straight to the bow, threaded through the men, and opened that bag. I saw something flash and realized it was our butcher knife.

There was a loud pop and a kerplop, a big splash, and one hundred thousand dollars in bullion was diving on its way to the bottom. Frayed rope waved in the air. It happened so quick that the men didn't realize it for a second.

Mama was already walking back toward Teetoncey when Hardie Miller gasped, "Gawd-almighty."

I felt somewhat the same myself, staring down as we passed over a crown of saltwater belches.

15

~~~~~~

IN A MOMENT, there was shouting from the life-saving boats and all the surfmen stopped rowing to look at that forlorn, empty line going to and fro in the sea breeze.

Hardie Miller yelled over to Filene in anguish, "Rachel cut it!" I thought he'd either weep or bash Mama.

Filene was now standing in the stern of the Heron Head boat, openmouthed. I thought he would roar. Instead, he squeezed out, "I don't believe it."

In the boats they were all stunned.

Suddenly, people on shore began hollering, observing that the chests were no longer hanging like big tubers beneath the oak jacklegs. I was told later that they thought some fool fisher hadn't tied them off properly.

Worst of all was the barge itself. All the men were yelling at Mama, circling around her like a pack of coon dogs. Some were jumping up and down. Some were pounding their fists. A few were looking down over the stern to spot the chests, a hopeless endeavor in ninety-odd feet of water. We had been passing over a trench.

In a pure daze, and doing my duty as the only male O'Neal on the barge, I finally stood by Mama and Teetoncey, not really convinced that I'd seen her slash that line. Also, I wasn't at all sure I should own the Widow O'Neal at this point. I glanced at Tee. Her face showed fright, understandably. This kind of thing probably did not occur in Belgrave Square.

I remember Mama sat there like a statue, very straight, not really letting her eyes focus on any of them. She was looking everywhere but at those men. The shawl was pulled tight around her head; her muddy garden boots stuck out from her long skirt. She coughed now and then but plainly, nobly ignored them. That butcher knife was across her lap. It had a mean blade. Why, I thought, she's as tough as any of them.

"Woman, you have to be crazy," Hardie Miller frothed, as one sample. There were others. Equally disparaging.

Mama finally spoke to them, matter-of-factly. "That money belonged to this lil' girl, an' not one o' you thought anythin' but miserly. An' the people on shore jus' wanted to git their hands on it. Not for Teetoncey, though."

"But, Rachel, you had no right," shouted the usually calm, kindly Mr. Burrus.

Mama replied evenly, "The sea giveth an' the sea taketh away . . ."

That did not quite make logic since Rachel O'Neal was not the representative of the sea by any means.

Old-time wrecker blood curdled as we drifted in confusion for another ten minutes.

When the barge was beached, there was great

babbling while the people onshore tried to find out exactly what had happened to the bullion. Meanwhile, I was helping Mama and Tee down.

Mama didn't seem disturbed at all. She said to me, "Let's git Fid an' go home. We accomplished what we set out to do, thank the good Lord."

Go home, if we can get there, I thought. Lynching was not unknown in North Carolina.

The British consul ran up. He was livid. Before he could even sputter, Mama fixed him with a "Good day, sir." She was still holding the butcher knife.

Then Filene, having disembarked, tromped up. With wonderment, he said, "Rachel, you did not do that on purpose?"

"I sartainly did," said Mama, very unflinching.

Before Filene could speak again, the U.S.A. Treasury man charged in. They were coming from all directions. "I'm going to have you arrested," he said, as frothing as Hardie Miller.

The keeper blinked. Immediately putting his hands on his hips, Filene said, "Say again!" That blockhead went forward like a pecking rooster.

The U.S.A. man repeated, though not as forceful, "I'm going to put this woman in jail for destruction of federal property."

Suddenly, it got so quiet on that beach that you could have heard two feathers colliding. All the Bankers started coming up, even Hardie, moving in close to Filene and Mama. In a few seconds, that fancy-dressed government man found himself completely surrounded by surfmen and fishers, most of them six feet tall and not a twinkle in any eye.

I do not think that mainlanders really understand us. That poor U.S.A. man just didn't know how to figure this situation. He'd heard everybody else raging at Mama.

Filene said quietly, "This is John O'Neal's widow."

Enough of that subject.

Mama smiled knowingly at Teetoncey and myself. "Ben, Teetoncey, come go home with me."

She gathered her skirts and off we went.

A while later, Cousin Filene and Jabez came up to the house. They were both laughing. Filene said, "Rachel, now that I've had time to sort it all out, I was never prouder o' you than this afternoon."

I felt the same myself. I was just as proud of that woman as I'd ever been of John O'Neal.

Many people came by during the late afternoon and early evening to talk and laugh. We come to find out that Mama and Tee had put their heads together the previous day and decided to send that silver to the bottom for many reasons. The women couldn't get over Mama sitting on that fish box with a butcher knife instead of a Bible on her knees. They were tickled about that.

Everybody also enjoyed the part about Filene and the U.S.A. Treasury man, when Filene said, in a muted foghorn voice, "This is John O'Neal's widow." That man wilted in his pants.

It was told and retold.

What it really was—Mama had prevented us Bankers from making fools out of ourselves over a lot of silver.

What a time.

16

BUT THAT PROUD, raw, and interesting day on the *Shallowbag Beulah* took its toll. Mama's cold got worse and her cough deepened. She had chills and fever, and Sunday morning, four days later, she said, "Ben, I got to stay in bed. You fix the food."

Tee got some cold water in the sink bucket and began to change rags on her forehead every hour, but by noon, her breathing was very harsh.

I rode over to Heron Head and asked Filene to call Doc Meekins and then come over himself.

He called right away, but Meekins was up in Elizabeth City for the weekend, probably gambling, and wouldn't be back until Monday. With his own doctor bag and medicine book, Filene returned with me.

He talked briefly to Mama, and then used his stethoscope to listen to her lungs. In the front room he said, "Ben, she's not good. Go tell Jabez to call Hatteras Station. Have Mis' Mehaly ride up with whatever she's got for pneumonia."

Pneumonia.

"She took a penetrate this morning, Cap'n," I said.

Filene nodded. "I'm gonna give her somethin' now, too. But Mis' Mehaly may have somethin' else. It's hard pneumonia, Ben, and that means we got to fight."

I rode over to Heron Head, and then came back, going in to see Mama. Her breathing was harsher than before. Her eyes were dull from fever.

She studied me a moment and then tried to smile. She said, "I tol' you 'bout that ocean." She'd never give up hating it. Never.

Mis' Mehaly arrived at dusk and took over, going straight to the kitchen to get a pot boiling. She had several jars of liquid and some powder in a square of newspaper.

I said to Tee, "I'd just as soon have her over Doc Meekins. She'll put Mama on her feet by midweek."

Mis' Mehaly fussed around in the bedroom awhile, back and forth to the kitchen; then she came into the front room and said to us, "She'll sleep comfortable awhile. But I got to bring that fever down. She's got lobar pneumonia, I think."

Filene said, "I'll try to git a call through to Elizabeth City. Mebbe Doc'll have a suggestion."

Filene left about the time Mis' Scarborough came in with some hot food. She served it up to Mis' Mehaly, Tee, and myself; then sat down in our rocker chair. "I'll jus' sit awhile," she said, and began to rock.

The night was long. I looked in on Mama now and then. She slept but the breathing was labored. Mis' Mehaly scarcely left the bedside, then only to get more cold water and change the rags on Mama's forehead and wrists.

Tee went to bed about midnight and I fell asleep a little later on the couch, listening to the creak of the rocker chair. I felt Mis' Scarborough covering me but didn't say anything.

The women began to come over in the morning. Mis' Gillikin, Mis' Burrus, Mis' Farrow, Mis' Fulcher, who took the Bible and put it up against Mama's side. Then Filene arrived to say he hadn't been able to locate Doc Meekins.

Most of that Monday is a blur. I sort of wandered around, in and out of the house, not knowing quite what to do while she just lay there, eyes closed and gasping for air. The women talked softly.

Tee didn't quite know what to do, either. She kept saying, "Ben, she'll get well. I know she will."

I had my doubts.

Just after dark, Tee and I were sitting in the kitchen when Filene came in. He said, "Ben, you should come."

Tee followed me into the bedroom. Mama was so white, so still. Yet her breath rattled on, though it was weak.

I asked Mis' Mehaly, "Is she . . . ?"

Mis' Mehaly nodded.

I looked up at Cousin Filene. "What's the tide, Cap'n?"

He had to force his words. "It's on the ebb, Ben."

Death always came to Bankers on an ebbing tide.

I started to lift the covers. Mama had once said that she would have kept Papa and Guthrie alive by rubbing their feet; that a person needs a comforting hand. They reach out for help.

No sooner had I touched the quilt than Filene said, "No, Ben. She's gone loo'ard."

The breathing had stopped.

As I ran out of the room, the women began coming in to do what they had to do. I heard Teetoncey crying and calling after me but I didn't heed her.

I got Fid and rode off into the night, galloping wildly, feeling like I was going off like a flare. In all the time I'd known her, I'd never told her I loved her. But I had.

Far down the beach, almost to Big Kinnakeet, I jumped off Fid and put my head up against his sweaty neck and did explode.

Soon, I felt something around my legs. It was a panting Boo Dog. Somehow that dog knew. Somehow he knew. I knelt down.

I won't dwell longer here. It still hurts me.

The next day, we buried Mama in the Chicky graveyard, near the crosses with *A* for Appleton on them, Keeper Midgett reading the usual services from the surfman's manual.

I stayed at Heron Head Station for most of the next two weeks, sleeping upon a cot with the surfmen. Eating with them, and they didn't charge me a thin dime. Teetoncey stayed with Mis' Scarborough, everyone feeling it wasn't right for us to live in the O'Neal house together. I was at a loss in that house, anyway. But I saw Tee every day.

On the second day, we sat on the dock in the winter sun. Teetoncey asked, "What will you do now, Ben?"

"I'll go to sea, of course. Those were my

plans." But I had not intended them to work out this way. "I'll go to Norfolk and ask around at the ship chandle houses for a cabin boy's job. Just the way Reuben did." He'd gone to sea just after his thirteenth birthday and mine was only a few weeks away.

"Ship chandle?"

"Suppliers. Or I'll just walk along the docks and ask every mate I see."

"And you'll leave this house?"

"Why, sure. Nobody'll ever bother it. Some of the women will dust now and then, I expect. Reuben'll be home after his voyage."

Then Teetoncey said a foolish thing. She said, "Ben, why can't you and I live here together."

"You mean, get married?"

"Why not?"

I wasn't about to do that. I had no intentions of being a father by the time I was fourteen. If ever. However, I did not want to hurt her feelings. I said, "I don't think it's legal. There's not a preacher in all North Carolina who'd marry two younguns together."

Tee sighed. But it was a nice thing for her to suggest.

"Anyway," I said, "you've got to go back to London and run your own house."

The consul had notified Filene that he wanted her to come to Norfolk on the railroad the following week. Although she was welcome to stay at the Scarboroughs, I think she was ready to go. There comes a time when you have to go from one part of life to another. It was about now, for both of us.

Tee said, "Ben, what will you do with Fid and Boo Dog?"

I'd been thinking about that. "Fid can take care of himself. These tackies have been out here for a hundredfold years. He feeds himself in the marsh. But I'm sure Jabez will check on him occasionally. Ride him now and then to make sure he doesn't go wild."

"How about Boo Dog?"

"Well," I said, "I was thinking you should take him, if you will. He has sure taken to you, and his gold coat goes with your hair."

She got all watery eyed.

I said, "How about it?"

"I'd like that very much."

So that was settled. We walked on toward the Scarborough house. Midway, she put her hand in mine. I left it there.

The next week, Tee packed what few things she had and along with Boo Dog, we departed Chicky dock in a sharpie, with Jabez at the tiller; Mark Jennette as crew. A lot of people were there to see her off, this castaway girl having caused quite a stir on the Outer Banks. Everyone was fond of her.

We jabbered back and forth at each other all the way to Skyco where we'd meet the *Neuse,* the white steamer with "Norfolk & Southern R. R." painted on its side. The *Neuse* would get her to Elizabeth City by 10 A.M. the next morning to catch the train.

At Skyco, we all boarded the steamer. Those are nice ships with a spacious foredeck and benches to sit on; four lifeboats and a big raft. She'd be safe as Boo's fleas on that ship for the inland passage. Food smells came out of her galley. Candy and apples were for sale.

When it was time to go, she went to the head of the gangway with me. I said good-bye to Boo Dog, and then stood up.

She said, "Ben, I love you."

I said, "I love you, too," without flinching a fraction.

Then she kissed me full on the lips. That wasn't at all bad. That girl had surely mommicked me.

Then Jabez, Mark, and myself waited on the dock while the vessel's lines were being slipped.

Tee called down, "Write to me, Ben."

I promised I would.

Then Boo Dog put his paws up on the rail and started barking his fool head off at me.

I said to him, "Have fun in London, you crazy hound." Wouldn't you know he'd get to see the world before I did.

The *Neuse* sounded her whistle, breaking the quiet of the sound country, raising ducks and gulls; then backed out toward the channel. Soon, smoke puffing from her high stack, she was headed north for the Pasquotank River and Elizabeth City.

So the girl with the pointed nose and daisy yellow hair departed, along with a former Carolina duck dog.

We went on back to Chicky.

A week later, it was time for me. I stitched up a good seabag from canvas Filene gave me and packed it, and then wrote a letter to Reuben, leaving it on the doily edge by the lamp on the oak table in the living room. I told him what had happened to Mama and that I was headed for sea at last. I said I'd keep a watch for the *Elnora Langhans* and if we ever passed it close aboard under full sail I'd give him a big hello.

I signed it, "Love, Ben." Not just, "Your brother." Mama would have been proud of that.

I said good-bye to Fid, and then stood at the end of our path and looked all around. There was beauty in this rugged land. I just hadn't seen it before. I'd be back.

With my kit, I went on to Chicky dock. Everyone for miles around was there. Kilbie, Frank, the Gillikins, Farrows, Fulchers, Midgetts, Gaskinses,

Burruses, Grays, O'Neals; all the surfmen. They made over me and wished me luck. Another son of the Outer Banks was off to sea, for better or worse.

Then Keeper Filene Midgett himself got into the sharpie, along with Jabez. That was quite an honor for the surf captain to escort me. We shoved off, caught the breeze, and laid knots on toward Skyco.

On the way, smoke winding off his pipe, Cousin Filene said, "You'll do real fine, Ben."

"You sure will," Jabez agreed.

I thought so, too. I didn't look back.

Adventure on the high sea . . .

The Odyssey of Ben O'Neal

THE CONCLUSION
OF THE CAPE HATTERAS TRILOGY

Ben and Teetoncey take to the sea—he, to find his brother, and she, to escape a forced return to England. But can they survive merciless storms, the harsh realities of ship life, and a relentless pursuer?

Turn the page for the first chapter of
The Odyssey of Ben O'Neal . . .

I

THERE IS A trusted saying on our remote Outer Banks of North Carolina that we who live there are all frail children of the moody Mother Sea, that she watches over and controls our every destiny. Shapes us as she carves out sandbars. Puts us in raging waves or calm, sunny waters. Makes fools out of us now and then, and isn't beyond having a good laugh herself. However, in her behalf, the old people claim she takes a long and careful time before making up her mind on how to dispose of us. She'll beckon us mysteriously when she's ready and not a tide before. There is also steadfast belief from Kill Devil Hills clear to Hatteras village and Ocracoke Island that she talks to us constantly and often we don't listen.

I do believe that now, although I didn't pay it much attention in March 1899, when my various voyages began. The Mother Sea was having a good laugh for herself during that trying period.

In the chill, gray dawn of a Tuesday, in the midmonth, sun reddening but not yet mounting the horizon, I stood at the dew-coated rail on the quivering stern of the steamer *Neuse*, looking south down Croatan Sound, which lies between Roanoke Island, of Lost Colony fame, and the flat, marshy Carolina mainland. Below my feet, glassy bubbles and white froth boiled out from the railway ferry as she throbbed steadily toward the Pasquotank River and Elizabeth City, North Carolina, where a train would be waiting to carry me on to Norfolk, across the Virginia border.

A knowledgeable but plotting girl once told me my face smacked poetically of sun on Irish bogs and Land's End winters. I can't at all vouch for that, but I can tell you how I looked that Tuesday otherwise. I was clad in a sturdy brown wool jacket, good knickers, black stockings without holes in them, and a seaman's blue wool cap (courtesy of surfman Mark Jennette), and by my legs rested a tubby canvas bag containing clothes, a pair of rubber boots, writing paper, a towel, and a bar of soap. So far as I knew, I was well equipped for what lay ahead but not so well off for what lay behind.

Way down the sound I could still make out the little boat's sails but could no longer see the comforting, hunched forms of Keeper Filene Midgett and surfman Jabez Tillett. Already they were beating away in the sharpie, and in late afternoon would arrive at Chicky Dock, on the Pamlico Sound. The Outer Banks, a string of small islands with low dunes and hammocks, bent oaks and scrub holly, flank the sounds, with a watching and listening and talking Atlantic Ocean on the other side, to east. Without doubt, Filene and Jabez would be safely to home at Heron Head Lifesaving Station, which Keeper

Midgett commanded, well before supper of wild pig or Mattamuskeet deer or roast ruddy duck, over which to talk about the event of the morning: my great departure.

Home, I couldn't help but think. With people they knew. Places they knew. Standing there, I shivered, I remember, and it wasn't from any icy wind. Disgraceful tears, once more (and I was certainly glad that the men in the sharpie hadn't seen them), had stopped. I'd resolutely fought them back, but somehow my throat kept on crowding. Only ten minutes before, when the *Neuse* pulled away from the dock at Skyco, Filene and Jabez had let the sharpie drift on out into the channel, then waved a last farewell before hauling sail up.

Never would they know just how close I'd come to yelling, "Take me with you."

A few minutes later, with three miles of brown water already separating the sailboat from the high-stacked white steamer, I thought very hard about turning myself around in Elizabeth City, swallowing my pride as I was gulping the gummy throat lumps, admit I was scared right down to my high-top shoes. Go home and unpack my seabag and wait in the small shingle house near Heron Head for brother Reuben to return from his voyages in the Caribbean.

I also distinctly recall hoping I'd see that sharpie come smartly about and race after the *Neuse,* finally catching it in Lizzie City, big Cousin Filene shouting up, "I been thinkin', Ben. You ought to wait to next year, when you're fourteen. Come on down an' git in this boat with us . . ."

It didn't happen, of course.

Then I tried to imagine what they were saying to each other and later found out I wasn't the width of six hairs off.

FILENE: "I do deceive that boy may be tougher'n John O'Neal. Didn't leak nary a tear. Jus' stood there manly an' said good-bye. For sure, he is tougher'n Reuben. Why, the night his mama died, if he cried I didn't see it. He jus' took off south on that pony o' his."

Well, I cried plentysome.

FILENE: "But a dozen times this week I felt like tellin' Ben he shouldn't go. Too quick after his mama died. Too soon to git his feet wet. He should stay with us up to the station, or up to the Odens or Farrows or Gillikins, an' they all thought about offerin'. . . ."

I would have refused and they all knew it. I'd talked too bragging much about going out to sea; dug my own foolish pit, so to speak.

FILENE: "Thirteen's a mite young to go to open sea, but Ben could always rightfully tell us that his brother had done it no older'n that. Others on the Banks afore him."

JABEZ: "That is true, Cap'n. I did myself." Jabez often took a big spit of Ashe's best plug after he said something profound and undoubtedly did this time.

FILENE: "As I do recall, Reuben was not a month over thirteen when he went off to Norfolk. I remember that Rachel, God rest her soul, was beside herself."

JABEZ: "That she was. I don't think it happened more'n a year after John O'Neal capsized."

FILENE: "About then. But I think John O'Neal, God rest his heroic soul, too, would have been right proud today that he had a boy who'd buried his dead an' faced the wind."

JABEZ: "Right proud." And then a six-to-eight-foot spit.

In truth, I wasn't facing the wind, and the region between my chin and forehead must have looked like a wrung-out mop.

I stayed by the rail until the peak of canvas vanished behind the first sun rays and then made my way toward the bow, pausing outside the lounging and dining saloon. It was richly carpeted in red, everything clean and shining. Forward were two long tables with snowy cloths, silver-colored cream pitchers, and thin little rose vases, minus roses because it wasn't summer as yet.

Other passengers were already eating breakfast. The coffee smelled good, as did the frying pork belly. So, carrying my seabag inside, placing it down where I could watch it—Filene had warned of thieves north of Kitty Hawk—I advanced on one table and sat down at the far end, away from other diners. Looking around that saloon, I'd never seen such splendor.

In a moment, a tall, elderly waiter in a starched white SS *Neuse* jacket with brass buttons on it placed a glass of water in front of me and said pleasantly, "Mornin'. We got some nice Smithfield ham today. Or some Philadelphy scrapple. Virginia trout. Grits 'n' gravy."

From strain, my voice cracked when I answered. "Reckon I'll have some oatmeal, please." More and more, my vocal cords were doing that of late, the usual plague of change of life.

Almost without thinking of it, I touched my pants pocket to see if the odd change was still there; let my hand slip stealthily to my breastbone to feel the fourteen dollars, my entire fund, bound tightly and hanging on a whistle lanyard, an idea of Filene's. It was safely there.

I'd seen these steam railway ferries many times as they plied the sounds and had boarded this same vessel once, just recently, when delivering Teetoncey, the British shipwreck survivor who'd lost her parents and was headed back for

London, England. But I'd never been a passenger myself and had no idea what they charged for breakfast. Oatmeal shouldn't be more than a few pennies, anywhere.

"No ham 'n' eggs?" asked the waiter, tempting me.

"Just some oatmeal, please," I replied, feeling hot and stuffy.

"Shame we got no berries today," said the waiter, moving off toward the galley.

Thirty minutes later, I was down on the second deck of the *Neuse*, leaning out of an open cargo port near the stern, throwing up. There was hardly a ripple on the Albemarle Sound and I could only guess that the sour gush of porridge wasn't exactly from seasickness.

Theodore Taylor

Acclaimed author Theodore Taylor was born in North Carolina and began writing at the age of thirteen, covering high school sports for a local newspaper. Before turning to writing full time, he was, among other things, a prizefighter's manager, a merchant seaman, a movie publicist, and a documentary filmmaker. The author of many books for young people, he is known for fast-paced, exciting adventure novels, including the Edgar Allan Poe award winner *The Weirdo; Air Raid—Pearl Harbor!;* and the bestseller *The Cay,* which won eight major literary awards, among them the Lewis Carroll Shelf Award. Mr. Taylor lives near the ocean in Laguna Beach, California.